7 Steps
To Self Mastery

EVERYTHING STARTS IN
THE MIND

JACK MAKANI

First Published in May 2019

ISBN: 978-93-5347-484-3

BLUE ROSE PUBLISHERS
www.bluerosepublishers.com
info@bluerosepublishers.com
+91 8882 898 898

Cover Design:
Srijan Bandyopadhyay

Typographic Design:
Teena Maurya

Distributed by: Blue Rose, Amazon, Flipkart, Shopclues

ABOUT THE AUTHOR

The author **Jack Makani** has experienced a big shift in his own life. Born in Denmark in 1943, he led a totally ordinary life serving as major in the Danish Army. An unexpected divorce at the age of 46, initiated his existential and spiritual quest. He gave up his military career to became a healer and a trainer in personal development. At that time he also became aware of a dream he had in his mind – that he would become one of the trainers travelling all over the world teaching people how to achieve the dream of their life. Today he has fulfilled that dream. Having become one of the world's best known trainers in personal development, **Jack Makani** now lives a "life on the road" – teaching people exactly what you are holding in your hands now – the practical tool of how to turn the dream of your life into reality.

You can read more about Jack Makani and his trainings on *www.makani.com.*

SELFCOACHING: THE 7 STEPS TO YOURSELF

We are all creators of our life whether we like it or not. This is the basic assumption behind this book. The famous author Deepak Chopra claims that "the world is inside us". When we understand that, we start to get in touch with the tremendous power that exist inside human beings. This book reveals the practical steps of how you can guide yourself to achieve whatever is important to you. The book is divided into 7 chapters or 7 practical steps. The steps are:

1. Take responsibility for everything in your life

2. Know yourself

3. Explore the present

4. Clean up your life

5. Live from the heart

6. Decide what you want

7. Empower yourself

The book is full of very practical tools and processes leading you through the steps. You can make the process even more intensive by adding the supplement: the videos with demonstrations and further explanations and the audios with special trance inductions assisting the unconscious expansion of your personal resources. You also have the opportunity to download a free writing manual for all the exercises. Do you need to do this 7 step process only once in your life? Probably not. We are living in a world changing rapidly because we are changing inside ourselves. And you may need sometimes to go back and redo the process, also as a way to make it clearer to yourself what is going on in your life and inside your own personality.

PREFACE

I remember an event in August 1999. I was standing in a hotel lobby in Sydney, Australia trying to connect my laptop to the Internet using a small mobile device. However, it wasn't really the Internet – it was the IBM World Wide Net, the Internet was not commercial at that time. It took me two hours to get that connection and mail my office in Copenhagen. I mention this because that occurred just over a decade ago and can today we are expect to be online all the time.

During these last fourteen years we've had an amazing technological revolution and we might ask ourselves, 'What will be next?' My guess is that we are approaching a comparative revolution of the human mind; that the mind of coming generations will be able to do things we can hardly imagine today.

So what is going on at the moment? Some people speak of a tremendous psychological transformation. others offer a more spiritual explanation and refer to the end of the Mayan Calendar. Some people suggest there is a new kind of human species being born at the moment – the Indigo or Crystal children while others propose an astrological perspective to the changes taking place. Some people see God behind it and there are still others proposing many other kinds of explanations.

So what is the truth? I learned a principle from shamanism years ago: "The World is what you think it is". This gives us the freedom to find our own explanations. Personally, I see a tremendous shift in human consciousness taking place. The question is where will that take us? We don't know for sure, because nobody can really predict the future; the future is a consequence of the decisions we make in the present.

However, I think we will discover that we have the freedom to create whatever we want in life and at the same time, we will realize that we need to take responsibility for that. You and I, together with everyone else, can create something totally new. Whatever this new era is really about, it seems to offer us the opportunity to become masters of our own destiny.

Many people have not noticed this yet; they continue to live as they have habitually done in the past, which is understandable. Much of our belief system has been passed down through the generations from a time in history where we were bound by duty and had little personal freedom. That said, we all need to discover the opportunities of the new time.

I have been teaching Neurolinguistic Programming (NLP) for many years. It is an amazing model and I owe much of my knowledge to it.

At some point in my journey, I encountered the following quote from Aristotle, a Greek Philosopher (384-322 BCE): "Educating the mind without educating the heart, is no education at all."

I realized that I needed to expand my teaching further and so created Self-coaching which, amongst other things, includes the idea of mindfulness.

Self-coaching is a self-analysis process for embracing new possibilities. It is a manual for the Self. Based on my 24 years of experience in "Creating the life you want", it has never been timelier than now. The future is now and the opportunities available to each and every person have never been greater.

The seven steps in this book are based on the idea that the mind is a hologram containing numerous options for each of us to master our own destiny. The seven chapters guide you through these steps:

- Take responsibility for your life
- Know yourself
- Explore the present
- Clean up your life
- Live from the heart
- Decide what you want
- Empower yourself.

The purpose of the Self-coaching process is to offer you knowledge and a number of techniques and methods that you can use to look deep into your heart and core values.

Self-coaching will help you decide what is right for you and will teach you to focus your mind towards that. It will also help you to clear up the fog of unhelpful thoughts and emotions stored in your mind. When you do that, you will discover that you truly are mastering your own destiny.

I have written this book in close collaboration with my beloved wife Helene Makani, who is an acknowledged international Enneagram expert and NLP Master Trainer. Many of the ideas and processes have been either inspired by or taken from her excellent NLP workbook. For that I am very grateful.

I would also like to thank all my students and colleagues who have assisted me over the years to understand the love, wisdom and power that exist in all of us. Without you I would never have been able to do it.

Good luck Jack Makani

CONTENTS

CHAPTER 1

TAKE RESPONSIBILITY FOR YOUR LIFE

....

You may have access to the Video and Audio pack which can be bought as supplement to the Self-coaching book. In that case I would recommend this for chapter 1:

Video: The World is inside. How to get a better internal state by simple anchoring. How to change the internal state by collapsing an old anchor.

Audio: General introduction. Explore the structure of the mind (submodalities). Introduction to positions. Creativity. Quiet Mind 1

....

I remember one of the key turning points in my life. It took place in January 1988 in Copenhagen, Denmark while I was a major in the Danish Army, working in the Headquarters of the Defence Forces. I had been married for 22 years but was recently separated from my wife. She had been participating in Gestalt therapy training and had realized that it was time for her to move on, so we formally separated and she moved out. Luckily our two sons were teenagers, almost able to take care of themselves.

However, the divorce shocked me and I began to review my life situation. I was no longer happy with my job as an army major, I found it increasingly tedious – and I had a growing sense that it was time for me to find something else to do for the rest of my life. The question, of course, was what? I applied for various management jobs within the private and the public sector with no result. So how could I find my new path?

Then one evening in January 1988, I went to a presentation about self-development. The speaker talked about taking responsibility for one's own life, in fact, he actually claimed that each of us is responsible for everything that happens in our life. I don't really remember the rest of the content, but that one sentence about self-responsibility stuck with me. I kept asking, 'Can that really be true?' It did not reflect my experience so far – I held many other people responsible for negative things in my life. In my mind, I had a list of people who had let me down, how could I be responsible for that? I got angry with that speaker for being so irresponsible as to mislead others with this kind of nonsense! It should be forbidden – society should not allow it!

Nevertheless, that sentence hung around in my mind. It was as if something in me knew it was incredibly important. Try as I might to push it away or forget it, I simply couldn't. It just kept playing on my mind so in the end, I decided to check it out. I enrolled on self-development seminars and then later I took my professional therapist training. It turned out to be exactly what I needed because during my training, I realised that the speaker in Copenhagen had been right. I came to understand that indeed, Each one of us is responsible for everything in our life, we have an inner world which we project outward and recognise it in the physical world. By doing that, we experience what we call reality. In the beginning, this was extremely abstract to me and it took me long time to really understand it. In a way though, it is simple enough: When I change my Inner world, Outer world as well changes and I become the creator of my reality.

This is what the chapter and rest of the book is about – looking deep into your Inner world and learning the psychological tools to adjust it. You will discover, as you move along the book and make changes to your inner life, your outer life will adjust to mirror it.

Then you will have revealed the most important secret of life to yourself, also you will know the most important secret of life. You have learned how you can create what you want in your life.

Let me tell you a story of Ivan Ivanov.

Ivan was born in St. Petersburg where he grew up in a small apartment with his parents and his six brothers and sisters. He left school early and started as an apprentice in one of the biggest bakeries in St. Petersburg.

Everything went well for Ivan, apart from the one thing: he thought one of the bakers was very unpleasant, in fact, Ivan thought that this person always picked on him, he was impossible to satisfy and forever scolding Ivan. After about 6 months it became too much for Ivan and he replied fiercely back. One angry word led to the next and suddenly he had crossed a line. The owner came, heard the other baker's explanation and sacked Ivan on the spot.

There was Ivan, standing in the street wondering what to do. He did not feel at all like going back to his parents so instead he took the night train to Moscow, and next morning he walked the streets looking for an opportunity. He came upon a sign in a bakery shop looking for an apprentice. He walked in, talked to the owner and got the job. All went well for a while, apart from the fact that the owner seemed to always be after Ivan, who found it more and more difficult to keep his anger in check. One fine day, Ivan exploded and vented his feelings in the owner's face. Ivan was sacked on the spot.

Again he stood in the street wondering what to do. He could go back to St. Petersburg or try to find a better apprenticeship. Ivan chose to go further east. He got on the train to Irkutsk and walked around in the strange city, looking for a job. Eventually he found a bakery needing help, and he got the job and was even allowed to sleep in a shed in the back. After some time history repeated itself, Ivan again spoke 'the truth' right in the face of the owner and got sacked.

Ivan continued to go east and eventually stood in a street in Vladivostok. He went down to the port and stood there looking out over the Pacific. It was totally calm and Ivan felt the sun warming his face while he stood there thinking about what to do next. He could try to continue on ship or he could stay in town. While thinking, he looked down into the water and saw his own face reflected there. Next to that he saw himself in Irkutsk and next to that Moscow, next to St. Petersburg, and before that as a big schoolboy. He suddenly saw how his problem with authorities had repeated itself over and over again through his life, all the way back to the time he had been very unfairly treated by his father. In that moment Ivan knew that he did not need to go any farther. What he needed was to travel into himself. He realised that since the time with his father, he had seen all authorities as unfair. And he realised that he was the one responsible for what happened in his life. For Ivan that was a mind blowing moment, as he suddenly realised that he could change his own pattern.

Have you been blaming other people for things? You probably have. Personally, I spent forty years of my life blaming others for things that went wrong for me. This is actually very common, most people do it. However, when we do, we make ourselves the victim of our circumstances. The consequence is that we lose power; we let others become the cause of our life. When we take responsibility, we start to reclaim our power – we become the cause of our lives.

The story of Ivan sums up one of the most important things in life; that in order to really make changes in our lives we must look into ourselves and change from the inside. The reality we experience is simply a projection of our Inner world – also known as our 'Model of the World'.

SECTION 1
THE MODEL OF THE WORLD

We humans do not experience the world as it is – we experience a *Model of the World*, or to use another expression, *we experience a map of reality*. Every road map mirrors only a part of the reality of the land, and in the same way, our inner map of the world is only a model of the outer world. This is the reason why two people often experience the same situation in different ways.

We receive on-going impressions – or information – through our five senses. But only a tiny fraction of that information reaches our conscious mind. We humans simply cannot accommodate the millions of bits of information we are bombarded with daily, so the information is "filtered" by our minds, which is deleted, distorted and generalized by what we see, hear, feel, taste and smell.

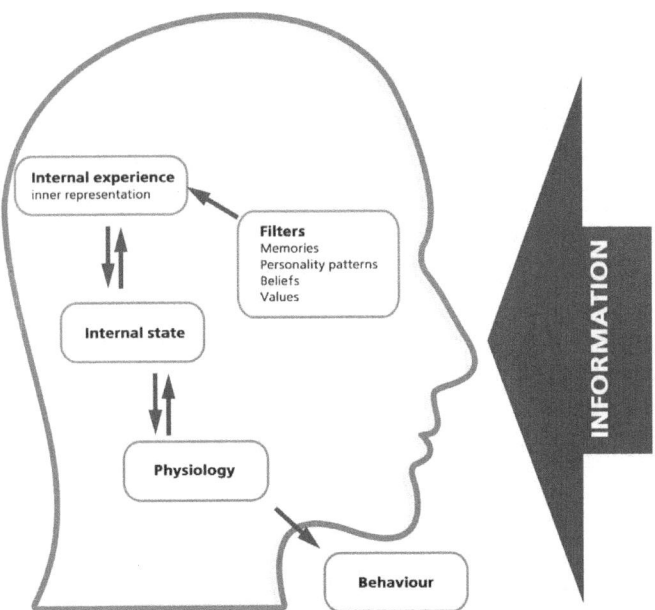

Figure 1

An example: When you stroll along a city street, looking at the shops, you notice many things in the shop windows. However, you probably look differently at the various outlets. In front of some stores you will stop and look more closely. others you look at more briefly, and others you just pass by. When you finish your city stroll, you will be able to remember much of what you have seen but there will also be much that you cannot remember. The fact that you don't remember does not mean that it was not there; it simply means that your inner personal filter has deleted it as unimportant.

This happens constantly with everything we experience; we notice only part of it while the larger part is overlooked or experienced differently from how it really is.

We experience the world through the sensory impressions we constantly receive, but only a very small part of this information reaches our conscious mind.

Between reality and the mind is a filter that determines what information gets through to the conscious mind. We call this filter as the Model of the World, i.e. a kind of internal map of how the world works. The filter is formed by our personality patterns, some genetic, some formed during childhood. By filtering reality we create an inner model of the world, which is the one we react to.

The information that passes through the filter is our interpretation, or internal representation of reality. Each piece of information 'represents' the external reality. We do not experience reality as it is, but as a personal, internal representation of it. The internal representation consists of internal images, sounds, words, body sensations, and possibly odour and taste.

An example: Maybe you can remember an experience of walking on a beach along the coast. You *see* the beach with seaweed and rocks in the sand and *see* the waves washing up the beach. You *hear* the sound of the sea from the waves lapping up on the beach and the *cries* of seagulls. You *feel* the warm sand beneath your feet and warm winds that caresses the skin. You *smell* the seaweed, which has rotted on the beach for a few days and you *taste* the saltiness from moisture in the air that touches your lips.

When you think back on the event, you may relive all this in a split second and acquire a happy inner feeling – noted in figure above as the internal state. Maybe you will then smile at a friend or start humming a particular tune – this is the reaction to the internal representation.

The process of linking the sensory representation together with an internal state and creating the meaning is referred to as anchoring. This is how we recognize something. For example, we talk to someone and unconsciously recognize their body language to be the same as one of our parents, triggering an anchor to be released and causing us to react to the person in a similar way as we do to our parent.

We unconsciously choose to represent an external event containing millions of bits of information in a simplified internal representation, and this is critical to how we experience the situation and what impact it will have on us.

Later in this chapter we will look more into how a filter is formed. In the following section the concepts of deletion, generalization and distortion are described.

Deletion

As already mentioned, our mind omits large amounts of information. According to modern science, our capacity is around 11,000,000 bits of information per second! The information is received through the nerves in the skin, through the eyes, ears, mouth and nose. However, scientists have proved that our Conscious Mind can only perceive between 16-40 bits of information per second. It is also known that we store significantly more than 16-40 bits of information in the Unconscious Mind – information that we can access through the techniques we will examine later. But still much is omitted. And the information that does come through is generally in keeping with the framework of understanding that already exists there.

You can read the daily newspaper thoroughly and still overlook certain articles, and you may even believe that those articles do not exist. But many people have experienced that if they have a new interest, for example trekking in Nepal, they suddenly realize how many articles and stories are there about Nepal and trekking out there. or people with a new born child find that the world is crowded with prams – where it definitely was not before!

Try to look around the room you are in right now and see it with the eyes of a real estate agent – what do you notice? Which details do you pay attention to? Next, imagine that you are a cleaning assistant and now you will probably pay attention to something else. And finally look round as if you were a 7 year old child – what do you notice now?

Generalization

To accommodate more information and to perceive new things faster, our mind generalizes large amounts of information. An artist or graphic designer can distinguish many shades of red, while most others generalize in pink, red and dark red. We recognize immediately 'man' or 'woman' at a glance. We categorize the 'young' or the 'old'. Similarly, we generalize from one or two events – if we, for example, burned our fingers on a candle when we were children, we know that another lighted candle will be hot. If we have been repeatedly scolded for being late for dinner, most people generalize that it is unpleasant to be late. Often this generalization is with us for the rest of our lives, long after we have grown up and there is no-one to scold us.

As mentioned above, the advantage of generalization is that it enables us to accommodate more information and perceive faster. On the other hand it also means that we may fail to see the individual behind the category, or we may generalize an experience to be always true. This is desirable when it comes to avoiding burns from a candle, but less useful for someone who gives a small, unsuccessful talk at a young age and from this generalizes that "I am a bad speaker!" Too often our mind functions this way, generalizing from one unpleasant experience to think that it will always be true.

Distortion

Apart from deleting and generalizing, our mind also distorts much of the information it receives. Distortion means that things are perceived differently than they are in reality. An example might be the bank cashier, afraid of a robbery, who "could clearly see that the bulge in the young man's jacket had the form of a revolver" – until he withdrew his hand from his pocket and opened his wallet. The bulge was distorted to have the shape of a revolver – and the cashier's anxiety was causing the distortion.

In general, communication distortion is a very common phenomenon. We think we know what others think or what their intention is in what they say, and thus we hear them say something other than what they are actually saying.

For example, take the man who says to his wife: "It really gets dusty quickly in summer" and she replies: "I don't want to bother cleaning today". He would be puzzled because he has not asked her to clean, he just commented on the seasons.

So what is this Model of the World?

The Model of the World is about how we communicate with ourselves and with our surroundings. It encompasses the relationship between our internal communication and the way we communicate with others. In other words, it is how our thoughts affect our internal state, and in turn, the way we treat other people. It determines how our thoughts affect the actions we take – or do not take. Our thoughts are the key to improving our daily lives and achieving our goals.

It all starts with how we think, how we create our own model of reality, and not least, how it is possible for us to change this model so it is more effective for us.

As you begin to perceive your life in a whole new way, you can increase your chances of getting more of what you desire whether that be a better job or increased success in the one you have, better relationships, more financial security etc.

The 'Model of the World' describes how communication takes place inside us in the form of the

- inner pictures that we see in our mind's eye
- sounds we hear inside our heads

- inner dialogue we have with ourselves
- body sensations and feelings we have

And how this inner communication influences the outer.

When we realize that we are responsible for our own life, we understand that in some way, reality is a projection of our `Model of the World`. It took me a long time to really understand this and when I finally did I realized how easy life is. If something unpleasant happened, I needed to look inside to identify the cause of it. I could identify the inner part of me or belief which caused the incident to show up in my life. That gave me a feeling of being in control of my life; I became the master of my own destiny.

This book is full of ideas, techniques and psychological tools for influencing your `Model of the World` and by doing so, you will unravel your hidden power. This is the key to understanding our opportunities, to realize that there are no limitations to human beings others than the boundaries we have created in our own mind.

Taking these steps will automatically lead to the unfolding of even more skills and resources that exist in your unconscious, benefitting yourself as an individual, your family and society as a whole.

How is the `Model of the World` created?

Our Model of the World is created partly from our genetic disposition and partly from experiences in childhood that left their imprint. Childhood consists of a long series of events that are experienced for the first time, often while the senses are completely open, leaving a profound imprint. What meaning we give to these events partly depends on our innate character traits and partly on how safe we feel and how our parents react (as they are our role models). Subsequent events are filtered through – and get their meaning from - those past experiences.

An example: A little girl sees a big spider and gets scared. Her mother sees the spider, screams and gets hysterical. The girl gets very scared because of her mother's reaction, which leaves a deep imprint on her mind, and she may, for the rest of her life, scream when she sees a spider – without really knowing (with her conscious mind) why.

The Model of the World (the filter) consists of:

- Memories
- Metaprograms/personality patterns
- Values
- Beliefs

Memories

Our memories are stored as images, sounds, words, body sensations and perhaps taste and smell. Part of our memories are known to us, others lie in the unconscious and appear as images, words, etc. without us being aware that we present them to ourselves. They can flash up inside the mind without us consciously noticing, causing us to react even though we are unaware why.

An example might be of a person going to sit for exam. An image of a previous exam that did not go well pops into her mind and triggers a feeling of incompetence and a certainty that she will fail. Her mind then distorts the words in the exam questions so that they are perceived as extremely difficult, decreasing her chances of passing.

Metaprograms / Deeper personality traits

Part of our filter consists of *meta-programs*, or deeper personality traits. Our meta programs determine whether we, for instance, experience the world mostly as a whole or in details; whether we rely primarily on our own or others' assessment of how well we have done; whether we are more aware of things that look the same or of what is different; or if we prefer that things stay the same to new things happening in life.

There are a large number of these meta-programs and they have great significance for our belief system. You can learn to hear another person's meta-programs, as they – like other parts of the filter – are reflected in the way the person speaks.

Values

Our personal values underlie in everything we do. They determine what we do, where we go, what we eat, whether we live alone or with others, what car we drive and whether we like watching TV or reading books – and *what* TV programs and books we choose. They are what motivate us to work or to do something else. Values are often unconscious, but you will easily find them by asking yourself: "What does it give me to do this? Why is it important? What is really important to me?"

Our values are personal, and many of them are formed during our upbringing and stay with us throughout life. Other values change with age, for example, at one time in our lives we may highly value going to a party and getting drunk every Saturday night, whereas later in life it is usually more important to be comfortable at home. Knowledge of people's values is extremely important in sales. In an advert, what kind of words will motivate people to buy?

Beliefs

Since we cannot experience the world as it truly is, we need to believe how it is and we do this by creating a series of beliefs about ourselves and what we are capable of, and about the world around us. We can distinguish between supportive beliefs that help us in our ability to achieve our goals, and limiting beliefs that inhibit us.

An example of a supportive belief held by a student may be: "I find it easy to learn new things", whereas a limiting belief could be: "I find it hard to learn".

Our beliefs are based partly on the Model of the World of our parents and other significant people, and partly on decisions we have taken in connection with childhood experiences. Many of them are closely tied to memories.

The Model of the World: A summary

As we have seen, the Model of the World is formed through our upbringing and the influences we have been exposed to. We each have our own internal Model of the World, each with our 'truth' about how the world works and this truth is based on our internal model.

Our internal memories, beliefs, values and meta-programs filter the information we receive so that the information fits with our internal model. This means that our experiences confirm what we already believe: if I think the world is a friendly place, I will focus on friendly people, and pay attention to them. If, however, I think the world is a hostile place I will be focusing on unkind people. The filter therefore determines how I sort reality. Our internal model can rarely be changed deliberately, as it builds on memories and decisions that have long been repressed to the unconscious mind. To make changes we must contact the unconscious, and this is exactly the purpose of the techniques you will find in this book.

Of the information we receive, we delete a portion, we generalize and we distort. What comes through the filter is called our internal representation, or internal experience of reality, or inner world.

This internal representation consists of internal images, sounds, words, body sensations and possibly smells and taste.

Section 2
Presuppositions

From our understanding of the Model of the World we can derive a set of assumptions which are useful to have in mind while working with the 7 steps program. You simply presuppose them in order to bring the techniques into action.

1.We do not experience the world as it is – we experience a model of the world. The map is not the territory

As shown in this chapter, we cannot experience reality as it is – we can only experience a model of the world. This means that every person's Model of the World, (whatever that person experiences) is only a model and not the whole truth. The good news is that we can change the Model if we are not satisfied with it. The moment we change our beliefs about the world, we change the way we perceive reality. This is what all change work or personal transformation is about.

2. Respect for other people's model of the world

Respect is not same as the acceptance. I can respect someone´s right to have a certain Model of the World, and when I do, communication with them will become easier. It is not always easy to take this presupposition to heart, particularly when dealing with people who have views that are completely different to our own. It can be explained with a quote from the philosopher Soren Kirkegaard: *"If one is truly to succeed in leading a person to a specific place, one must first and foremost take care to find him where he is and begin there".*[1]

1.Kirkegaard continues: "This is the secret in the entire art of helping. Anyone who cannot do this is himself under a delusion if he thinks he is able to help someone else. In order truly to help someone else, I must understand more than he – but certainly first and foremost understand what he understands. If I do not do that, then my greater understanding does not help him at all. If I nevertheless want to assert my greater understanding, then it is because I am vain or proud, then basically instead of benefiting him I really want to be admired by him. But all true helping begins with a humbling. The helper must first humble himself under the person he wants to help and thereby understand that to help is not to dominate but to serve, that to help is not to be the most dominating but the most patient, that to help is a willingness for the time being to put up with being in the wrong and not understanding what the other understands." Soren Kirkegaard, Danish Philosopher and Author in his book 'The Point of view for my work as an author', first published in Denmark in 1859.

3. I am the one who controls my mind and thus my results

Many people believe that it is someone else's fault that their life is like it is, or it is someone else's fault that they react the way they do. With this assumption we presuppose that we ourselves are responsible for everything that happens because our internal and external communication is what governs our life. If we are not satisfied with the response we get from others, or with our life in general, we are responsible for changing it by changing our Model of the World.

We can choose to follow in the footsteps of Ivan Ivanovitch throughout Russia – or we may choose to stop and look at ourselves.

4. There is no failure, only feedback

Many people are discouraged by things they do not succeed at – they see it as a failure, or perhaps even that they, as individuals, are failures. other people do not think in terms of failure, but take whatever happens as feedback that they can use for the next time, e.g., "Well, that didn't go very well, but I learned from it so next time I will do such and such instead". When we experience that everything is feedback, then we really have an opportunity to grow.

5. The meaning of your communication is the response you get. If you do not get the result you want, then change your communication

This presupposition is in line with no. 3 about the individual being responsible for his results and no. 4 on feedback. If, for example, you ask a friend to fetch a bath towel and he comes back with a tea towel, it means that you have not communicated "towel" clearly enough. Following this presupposition, instead of blaming the other, you can take responsibility for the communication and change it. With the self-coaching tools you can adapt your communication to suit the person you talk to. To understand what is being communicated, some people must have a visual image to connect to, others require a certain tone of voice to be used.

6. Every behavior has a positive intention

This presupposition can teach us to look for the intent behind what other people do, rather than just focusing on their behaviour. Maybe you don't like the flowers you receive but you recognize the intention behind the gift. Perhaps you don't understand why a person is violent, but you can ask yourself, 'What positive outcome is this person trying to achieve for herself here?'

When we start distinguishing between behaviour and intention we realise that our current behaviour or strategy of action does not always help us to achieve the results we want. Many of these strategies were adequate when we were children, but are not sufficient today. Too often we actually achieve the opposite of what we want. The Self-coaching tools allow us to update old strategies.

7. People already have all the resources they need to reach their goals

This presupposition is based on the idea that if you set yourself a goal which is really important to you, then you also have the capability of achieving it. Humans contain infinite resources, but many of these are not used because they are bound by inhibitory beliefs. The self-coaching tools can liberate those resources when we set goals for ourselves.

8. Flexible people and organizations have advantages over others

When you develop the ability to see other ways of doing things, you are more able to adapt to any situation. This applies to individuals who can adapt their communication to the person they are talking to and thereby get their meaning across. It also applies to organizations and businesses that are able to adapt to unforeseen situations and changing markets. One of the benefits achieved from the self-coaching tools is the development of a greater flexibility.

9. Accept who you are

We all have some core values which are so important to us that we will never let them go. One of my very deep core values is 'respect for other people' and this is so important to me that I can't imagine life without it. Who would I be then? Not me that's for sure. In other words, all of us have some values and beliefs which are so basic for us that they represent our identity. This may lead to reactions to and from other people that you don't like. A number of beliefs and reactions can be changed in the model of the world and some can't. The only thing you can do with your core beliefs and core values are simply to make a decision that they are okay for you. This is how you are. Learn to accept things the way they are within that area of your life. Learn to love yourself.

10. Any situation has several options. If something does not work – then do something else!

When we encounter obstacles, it is normal to either become passive or to do the same thing again, even if it did not work for the first time. If you develop a new habit of telling yourself that in any situation you have at least 3 options, then your mind will start to look for these options and suddenly you can choose between several possible ways to move forward. Start to look at obstacles in this way: "What are the three solutions to this?"

"If you do what you've always done, you'll get what you've always gotten."

SECTION 3

SUBMODALITIES – THE BUILDING BRICKS OF THOUGHTS

Now it is time to look closer into the structure of the mind – how are our thoughts organized?

We now know that our perception of reality is very subjective – a map of reality. Our next step is to look into how we actually structure this map or Model of the World in detail. So far, we have suggested that we store our experiences as internal images, sounds, words, body sensations, smells and tastes. That's the way we translate our senses to our internal representation. Now, we will explore more about what kind of mechanisms we use to construct these internal representations. The building bricks of the thoughts are called Submodalities. I think we will use the short version of this term and simply call them "subs" in this book.

These subs are very important for our internal model of the world, for how we recall memories, for how we imagine the future, in fact, for everything we think about.

Let us take an example: A man thinks that he must go out and dig the garden, but he gets tired at the mere thought. When he looks at the subs of his inner image, he discovers that he has made a huge dark image of the garden, with a very small version of himself standing in the middle.

He can now amend the image: making it brighter, adjusting himself to normal size, maybe adding some colour. The new image will make him feel much more motivated to get started.

It's not so much *what* we think of that's important, but much more about how we think of it. It is our inner model of the world that causes our perception of the outer world.

The internal model is in no way static. We can actually adjust it and this is very helpful for increasing personal motivation. The subs are the basic structure of our model of reality and how we organize them will create the inner states in the body making us feel motivated, unmotivated or just neutral.

I would like you to have your own experience with the following exercises. The purpose of these exercises is to give you an understanding of how you construct your thinking and how easily you can adjust it and still be you. You can do it alone or even better, you can ask a friend to take part.

Exercise 1:

Find a piece of paper and a pencil and think of something pleasant: a good friend; an animal you are very fond of; a beautiful sunset. See the picture in your mind's eye and allow the pleasant feeling to spread throughout your body, so you can really feel it.

Continue to look at the picture inside your mind's eye while you check the subs and write them on the paper:

- The size of the internal image
- Location in the field of view
- Distance from you
- Is it in color or black and white?
- Is it light or dark?
- Is it sharp or blurry?
- Is it like a movie or a still image (photo)?
- Is it 2 or 3 dimensional?
- Is it Framed or panoramic?
- Is it transparent or opaque?
- Does it have pastel or bright colors?

Looking at the picture in your mind's eye, slowly go through the list again and begin to adjust the subs. As the picture changes, notice how and when your internal state also changes. You can make the image larger or smaller. You can enhance the colors or make the image black and white. You can turn a movie into a photo, etc. Experiment with it.

You will find that by changing some of the subs you will change your inner state in your body. This means that you are able to deliberately affect your inner state through altering these subs in your inner representation.

Exercise 2:

Take pencil and paper and think about something you care less about. See it as an image in your mind's eye and notice the sensations in your body. Write down all the subs and check them in the same way as you did in exercise 1. Pay attention to the subs that change your inner state.

Exercise 3:

So far we have only dealt with the visual subs, so now let's explore some of the auditory subs.

Think of a person you like and look at them in your mind's eye. Now have the person speak to you inside your mind and listen to their voice. It may seem a little abstract but just imagine that you can hear the person speak to you.

Note the following:

- From where does the sound come (orientation)?
- Is it in mono or stereo?
- Do you hear it continuously or interrupted?
- What rhythm is there?
- Notice the words, whose voice is it?
- Is the tone high or low?
- Is the tone monotonous or melodic?
- How loud is the volume?
- Is it fast or slow?

Record the results of what you hear on paper. Then go through the auditory subs one by one and experiment by changing them in the same way as in exercise 1.

Exercise 4:

Think of someone with whom you have problematic communication. See the person in your mind's eye and listen to the person's voice. Find the subs and write them down on paper. Just use the visual and auditory subs that you have been using so far. Now start to change the subs and notice which ones change your inner state.

Exercise 5:

Think back to something that you like very much. Take plenty time to feel the sensation in your body and then explore what those body sensations are.

- Do you feel it a particular place in the body or all over?
- Is it stationary or in motion?
- Is it hot or cold?
- Is it continuous or interrupted?

Check out what happens if you change one or more of these body subs (Kinesthetic subs).

Exercise 6:

Think of something you greatly desire to achieve. In your mind's eye, visualize yourself in a situation where you have achieved it. Make it as visual as possible. Add some auditory subs too and experiment with the subs to find what makes it even more attractive for you to achieve this goal.

You can check the following:

- size
- color / black and white
- light
- sharpness
- film / photo
- words
- sound direction
- tone

Exercise 7:

Think of something that you do not really care about. It could be something that is part of your daily routine that you don't feel motivated to do. Find the single image which best represents this task. Now find the visual and auditory subs which are used to create this image and write them down.

Now think of something that you are really motivated to do.

Choose something that gives you such great pleasure that you are really motivated to do it. Now write down the visual and auditory subs from this image.

Now compare the subs from the two images – the motivated and the unmotivated. Identify the difference in the subs. Now check out what happens if you move the subs from the motivated image (only subs which are different) into the unmotivated image. You will probably find that this gradually moves your internal state towards being more motivated.

For example:

Not motivated	Motivated
small picture	big picture
grey	strong colors
fuzzy	fuzzy
dim	dim
photo	film
monotonous sound	range of tones
almost inaudible volume	normal volume

Differences
size
color
photo/film
varied sound
low volume

Let us state this one more time: It is not so much what you're thinking of (the content) but the way you think of it (the form) that causes your inner state. This means that by working on the subs you can influence your inner state and by doing that, you can also change the meaning.

I suggest that you go ahead and play with the different experiments and discover how you can change your inner state when you are dealing with people with whom communication is difficult for example, or how you can change your motivation for the tasks you have to do. It is not certain that you can change everything in your life this way; some things require more powerful techniques. You will find examples of these in the coming chapters.

People are different and we create our inner models of the world differently, all the way down to the particular subs that influence us most. It's very interesting to discover one's own personal subs i.e. which subs you have used until now to store bad experiences, and which you use to store the good ones, what subs make you more motivated to reach a goal and which will leave you unmotivated. You can learn what to say to yourself and what tone of voice to use when, for example, you feel insecure etc. Not least, you can discover how to move yourself into more resourceful inner states by adjusting the subs of your internal images to get the best effect.

In the following table, you can see an overview of the most common subs:

Visual subs	Auditory subs	Kinesthetic subs (body)
Size Placement in field of view Distance Color/ black-white Light/ dark Sharp/blurred Associated/dissociated Film/ still image 2- or 3-dimensional Framed/panoramic Transparent or dense Pastel colors/strong colors Focused/ blurred	Where does the sound come from? Are there words? outside/Inside yourself Where precisely? (right, left, forehead etc.) If it is your own voice: How old is it? Mono/ stereo Continuous/ discontinuous Rhythm Tone of voice (soft or harsh) Tonality: monotonous/ melodic Volume (loud or soft)	Location in body Hot/cold Relaxed/ tense Expanded/ compressed Intensity Pressure (hard or soft) Movement, shift Where does the movement/ change, originate and end? Continuous/ discontinuous The speed of the movement /change Weight (light or heavy) Texture (rough or smooth) Extent (how big)

Figure 2

It is not so much what you think of (content) as the way you think of it (form) that determines your inner state!

Section 4
Representational systems

As we have seen, each of us has our own internal representation of what we experience. We store our perception of what is happening now or what has happened in the past in an inner *representational system.* This can be abbreviated to: REPSYS

We can streamline the details of our REPSYS into four different REPSYS categories to determine whether an individual is currently thinking in mainly pictures, sounds, body sensations or internal dialogue.

- **Visual** – thinking in pictures
- **Auditory** – thinking in sounds
- **Kinesthetic** – body sensations, also including Gustatory – taste Olfactory – smell
- **Auditory-digital (Ad)** – words, meaning

Here are a number of examples of how a concept can be represented in the different four systems:

Visual	Auditory	Kinesthetic	AD
outline	talk about	go through	inform
unseen	unheard	tasteless	unacceptable
see	hear	feel	notice
overlook	overhear	pass over	ignore
look like	sound like	feel like	remind of
see	talk	meet	be contacted
look at again	talk about again	repeat	repeat
blind	deaf	insensitive	indifferent
symmetry	harmony	balance	equilibrium
looks bleak	rings false	weighs heavily	problematic
looks good	sounds right	feels good	optimistic
have an eye for	strike a chord	in my taste	sympathize

Knowledge of REPSYS can be useful in communication. E.g. If someone who mainly uses the visual system is talking to you, it is very useful to answer back using the visual system.

Exercise 8: which repsys are used in the following sentences?

Write V, A, K, AD

- The future looks bright.
- I can feel that I'm a bit out of touch with things now.
- Of course it looks different from his point of view.
- I find your reaction illogical.
- She could recall every word of our conversation.
- I think the way you talk to staff is unheard of in this company.
- Let's run through everything one more time.
- I think that her logical form is very sympathetic. 9.Your

Comment sounded just right, it was exactly what I needed to hear.

- I felt that I couldn't do anything else but follow my heart.
- I really tried to show who I was, but it was like I was completely overlooked by him.
- There was a great deal of information in your lecture.
- After the very fascinating lecture, there was a lengthy discussion.
- She looked radiant!
- Her words really struck a chord with the audience.
- The project was completed to the full satisfaction of the boss.
- The path is clear and I have a feeling that we can just go ahead, it will be quite easy.

SECTION 5
ANCHORING

Anchoring describes the process whereby an experience in the present triggers emotional states from earlier in our lives. These triggered inner states may be positive, such as when we hear a familiar tune and get in a good mood because it reminds us of something good from the past – or a 'negative' inner state, such as when we hear another song which reminds us of a bad experience. We can consciously use this knowledge about the links between sense stimulation and response to give ourselves or others access to resourceful states.

Most of us are familiar with how a certain smell or piece of music can trigger old memories. It is often referred to as association from one thing to another. We can also describe it as the 'stimulus-response model': a stimulus, such as a sound, triggers a certain response. Most people have heard of Pavlov's dogs, where the sound of a bell was linked to the smell of food. After a while the dogs began to salivate (response) at the sound of the bell (stimulus) even if there was no food.

In the same way, you may hear a song which reminds you of a certain holiday – and the sound of the melody alone is enough to trigger inner images of the beach, the atmosphere, the sunlight and the taste of your favourite food, or the wine…

We call this *releasing an anchor* – the song in the above example is the anchor that gives access to all the memories. So, an anchor is an element from a situation or an experience which makes the whole situation - and the emotions attached to it - emerge. Anchors are usually external, i.e. they come from outside stimulus and they trigger internal experiences/ responses. A siren, a church bell, an old photo, the smell of a damp basement etc. can take people back in time, and it happens unconsciously on a daily basis, for example when we react very emotionally to a particular comment from another person – it might just be that their tone of voice triggered a memory of us being told off at three years old!

Anchors can exist in any representational system and can

trigger all the other systems, for example, a specific smell (olfactory) can trigger old images (visual) of a childhood basement. A holiday photo (visual) can trigger taste experiences (gustatory) and the feeling of warm skin (kinaesthetic) and a particular piece of music that was played at the time (auditory). The different sensory impressions are anchored together and can mutually trigger each other.

This is largely used in advertising where certain pictures and sounds are presented in order to elicit good inner states in the viewer, thus creating the impulse to buy the product to achieve that inner state. For example, a commercial with beautiful, happy people triggers a state of (or a longing for) joy or happiness in the audience. The product becomes an anchor for the state and the next time the consumer sees the product, he/she associates it with this state and wants to buy it. The small melodies (jingles) that follow most commercials today also become anchors.

Even our language is an advanced anchoring process since either the sound or sight of a word can associate to particular thoughts and feelings in us. This is how words have meaning for us; they are anchored with certain pictures which in turn trigger the associated inner states. Just think of the word 'exam' which, for many people, is an anchor for getting nervous or tense.

In fact, all of our life is a constant anchoring process – we cannot avoid anchoring things together. We can take action to dissolve old anchors so that a certain word, picture or tone of voice no longer triggers an unwanted inner state and we can create new resourceful anchors through self-coaching. We can deliberately use anchors to get ourselves into useful inner states.

Now let's explore how we can form anchors that create access to new resources, i.e. anchor a picture, a sound or a touch to a resourceful inner state. This inner state can then be released whenever we need it – in other words, we can use it to remind ourselves of the resource.

One of the principles/presuppositions tells us that we have all the resources we need to reach our goals – the problem is that sometimes we get stuck because we cannot access the resource. Knowledge of anchoring can help solve this.

Exercise 9: Anchoring a Resource

This technique can be used for a situation where you feel a lack of personal resources. You may wish to have more calmness, power, self-confidence etc.

1. Think of a situation where you would like to have access to a specific resource. It could be when you are about to give a speech and would like to feel really calm.

2. Think of a situation from your past where you felt calm while you talked to a group of people. While you are immersed in the feeling of calmness, touch yourself somewhere specific on the body with one hand and keep it there for a short while.

3. Now think of another situation where you felt calm while talking to people. Again, once you are immersed in the calm feeling, touch yourself once more at the specific place, with the same hand, and hold for a short while. use the same pressure as the first time.

4. Now do this a third time with a third situation.

5. Now think of a future event where you are going to give a speech and associate into the situation in your imagination. Touch yourself at the specific anchor point with the same pressure and feel the calm as you imagine giving the speech.

6. When the time comes to give the speech in the future, touch yourself in the same way to release the feeling of calm right before you begin talking.

Exercise 10: Collapse an Anchor

This technique is used in situations where you have an unpleasant reaction to something and want to change it. For example, let's say you have a situation at work with a colleague who uses a particular tone of voice that causes you to lose your confidence. In fact, every time she speaks to you in this tone, your energy simply fades away. You can use this technique to resolve that.

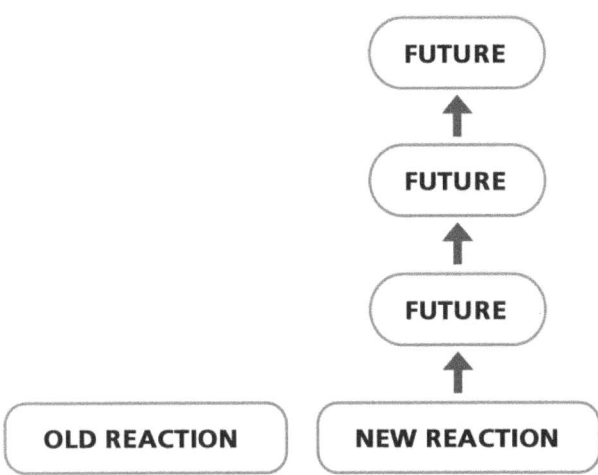

Figure 3

1. Take two pieces of paper and write *'new reaction'* on one, and *'old reaction'* on the other. Place them on the floor approximately 1 metre apart.

2. Step on the 'old reaction' spot and think back to the last time you had that unpleasant reaction to the colleague. Associate in so you can really feel how unpleasant it is.

3. Step back to a neutral place. Make sure that you have no feelings in this spot.

4. Now step on the 'new reaction' spot and imagine a situation where you are having a good or neutral reaction while talking to another person. Associate fully and stay for a short while so you really feel it.

5. Step out of this and become neutral again.

6. Step onto 'new reaction' one more time and think of another situation where you had a good or neutral reaction as you talked to someone.

7. Step into neutral again.

8. Repeat a 3rd time with 'new reaction'.

9. Now put the paper marked 'old reaction' below the paper 'new reaction'.

10. Step on the 'new reaction' paper and think about the colleague you used to react to. You will probably discover that the feeling has changed. If not, repeat steps 4–8.

11. Take a step forward into your future and experience how different it is going to be next time.

12. Repeat step 11 another two times, each time imagining a different scenario with that colleague, and experience the difference in your reaction.

Section 6
The Swish

This is a simple technique working with the subs. It is very useful when you have an inner picture that triggers an unpleasant internal state, particularly if the image regularly comes up for you and causes you discomfort each time. The swish gives you the opportunity to simply change the image for another that is more pleasant.

The idea of the swish is that the old picture releases the new picture, or in other words, we let the old picture function as an anchor for the new picture. It may sound a little abstract at first, but the technique itself is pretty simple.

For example, let's say you bite your nails and want to change that habit. The question you need to answer is: what happens when you feel the urge to bite your nails? Something happens inside – an image pops up at the unconscious level. That image is the key to using this technique. As soon as you identify the image, you can do the swish.

A swish can be used to change states of grief, guilt or other emotions that are linked to an old situation (an image in the mind) that is still tormenting you. You need to only find an image that is triggering the uncomfortable feeling.

For the technique to work it should be ecological for you, i.e. there should be no inner personality parts that want to hold on to that emotion.

When you do a swish, two things are important:
- You must insert a 'blank screen' in between the steps to ensure that the process only functions one way. This prevents the mind reversing the process at another time.
- The swish can be practised slowly at first, but then should be done very quickly so that the mind learns to process it so swiftly that the first picture is no longer visible.

The goal of the technique is that every time the unpleasant inner picture comes up, it is automatically covered by another, more pleasant image. After a while, only the pleasant image will be visible.

The technique is described step by step in the following exercise.

Exercise 11: Swish – the Technique

You can do this process yourself but you may find it easier to work with a friend. This description is for two people doing the technique; A is being guided by B.

1. B asks A to define the goal – what does A want to achieve? B asks A if he feels any internal resistance to that. Resistance will prevent the technique from working. If there is resistance, it will have to be resolved first. (this is discussed in chapter 4).

Unpleasant picture

Figure 4

Now B asks A to find the initial picture, i.e. the picture that releases the unwanted inner state. Then B asks A to put that picture out of his mind for a moment / think of something else.

2. Next, B asks A to create a supportive picture (see note below). Adjust the subs in this picture until A experiences a very positive inner state from looking at it.

Supportive picture

Figure 5

3. Now B asks A to make this supportive picture shrink to a small dot and then let it expand and fill the whole 'inner screen'. Practise this shrinking and expanding a few times.

Figure 6

4. Next, B asks A to place the little dot in the centre of the initial picture (from step 1), then let the dot expand to become a large, light picture totally covering the initial image.

Figure 7

1. B then asks A to imagine a 'blank screen'

2. A repeats steps 4 &5 three times quickly (so it expands like an explosion) and then anchors it into the future (referred to as 'future pace'). B can ask A to describe how it is different to think of the original image now. A continues until only the new, supportive picture is visible.

Notes on step 2:

The supportive picture should, of course, trigger a positive inner state. This image can be either an image of A in the future (dissociated), free from the problem.

For example, B can ask, – "What state do you want to be in?" or "How do you look now?"

This type of image is useful when A wants, for instance, to change a bad habit such as nail biting. The starting picture would be the bitten nails and the supportive picture would be A with longer nails and a good inner state or it can be some other image that generates a positive inner state, whatever A suggests.

If A is working with an unpleasant picture in connection with grief for example, the starting picture may be of the deceased in a coffin, and the optimal supportive image would be one of the deceased in a happy situation from his or his life.

Take responsibility for your life: A summary

In this chapter you have seen that you are in fact responsible for your own Model of the World, i.e. the way you think (your subs) and thus your own life. The question is whether you are willing to deal with this responsibility or ignore it. No matter what you choose, the responsibility is still yours, but if you ignore it you may become just a brick in someone else's life instead of creating your own.

For most of us it's extremely difficult to accept the idea that we alone are responsible for our life. Perhaps we can agree on certain areas, but others are harder to accept. We blame other people – our parents, husband or wife, even our children sometimes. We blame society, politics, our economy, health, resources, age, education etc. But blaming others (making yourself a victim) will only create more of what you don't want. This is because every time you don't take responsibility for your life, you give away your power and your opportunity to take action and change.

Exercise 12: Take Responsibility

I suggest you take some time to write down the situations and areas of your life where you have found it most difficult to accept the idea of taking responsibility. These are most likely the areas where you really have the opportunity to create the biggest changes.

Exercise 13: How did I Create that?

Write down 5-7 situations from your past where you did not achieve the result you wanted. Now analyze these situations, recording the decisions you made that created the negative results.

For example, imagine you had planned to run a marathon. You

started a training program and then halfway through, you suddenly quit. What happened? Were your values about the marathon in conflict with your values about how you spend your leisure time? Did you accidentally create a demotivating anchor? Were there sub conscious beliefs about your ability to achieve the goal?

What decisions have you been taking in your life that are really limiting for you? Are you willing to take responsibility for your life now and make new decisions?

Exercise 14: What do you know now?

What insights have you gained from reading this chapter?

What do you know about yourself now that you were not aware of before?

CHAPTER 2

KNOW YOURSELF

....

You may have access to the Video and Audio pack which can be bought as supplement to the Self-coaching book. In that case I would recommend this for chapter 2

Video: Johari Window

Audio: Expanding personal resources. Intro to Timeline Change

....

I started my therapist training in 1990. At the time I was still serving as a major in the army, so my studies took place during weekends and vacations. After about 6 months, I was jogging in a woods outside Copenhagen one day, it was autumn and the leaves were falling from the trees. Around me, all of Nature was changing its colors with the shades of yellow, brown and red all over. I began to increase my speed. My heart was beating fast and my clothes were soaked in my sweat. I tried to pace up as much as I could continue running. I didn't know why – it just felt right. Suddenly, I heard a voice in my head saying, 'It's now'.

Instantly, I knew what it meant. When I had started my therapist training, I had made a deal with myself that I would stay in the army until I received a signal to quit. However, now that I had my signal, everything suddenly seemed threateningly close. My mind started to come up with various arguments for not making the move: I did not have clients; I didn't have enough money; I hadn't finished my therapist training; I was not a psychologist; it would be better to wait and see. So many arguments and, in a way, they were correct. However, the voice I'd heard was very clear and had been followed by the most wonderful warm feeling in my chest, which I understood to be part of the signal. I reached home and wrote my letter of resignation letter to the army.

I had discovered something new about myself, something which may have existed inside me for a long time which had suddenly stepped forward and appeared in my conscious mind as a signal or specific understanding of what to do. A model exists to describe this phenomenon; it is called the window of Johari:

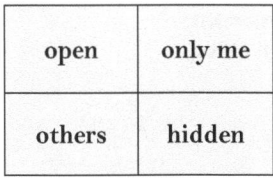

open	only me
others	hidden

Figure 8

'**Open**' is what I know about myself and what I let others see about me. This part of me is truly open to everybody. This area of my personality covers some of my thoughts and reactions with no secrets. There is a current trend of growth of this area amongst people, evidenced perhaps by the fact that so many people are sharing things about themselves on social media - things that were previously kept private.

'**Only me**' covers aspects of myself that I know about myself but choose to keep private, or perhaps share with only few selected people. I hold back because there are things here I don't like to show to others. It may be because they are embarrassing to me or somebody else.

'**Others**' contains other parts of my personality which I don't really know about myself. These may be those habits or reactions that I don't pay attention, to or things that bother other people without me being aware of them. We could call this area the "feedback" area; listening to others about this quadrant can be very useful.

'**Hidden**' refers to another area of my personality where there may be resources or talents that I am not aware of. These resources remain hidden until they are revealed from the unconscious, when the time is right. This is somewhat similar to what happened with me while running in the woods and having received the "go" signal.

It can be said that personal development is all about expanding the 'Open' area of our personalities.

There is an old Polynesian model called "The 3 Minds" which can also be used to describe this phenomenon:

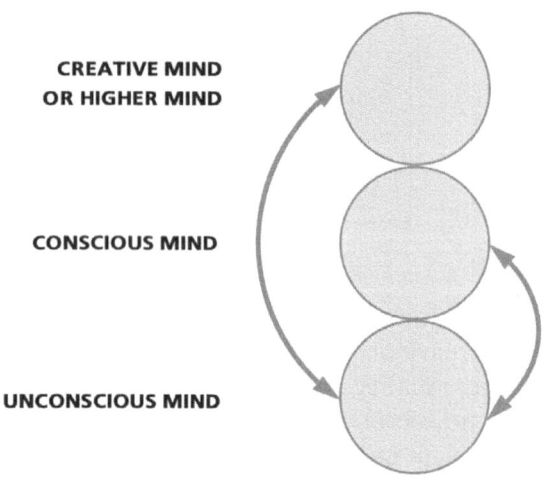

CREATIVE MIND OR HIGHER MIND

CONSCIOUS MIND

UNCONSCIOUS MIND

Figure 9

The idea of the three minds of Human beings can be found in most ancient teachings.

The **Creative mind/Higher Mind** is also called the higher intuition or higher Self and represents a kind of overview of your life and an understanding of who you are at the deepest level. It seems to be mainly situated above the head.

The **Conscious Mind** is in charge of decision making and the sensory system. It is in this mind we create meaning (which we do all the time). In this mind, we experience our inner world as pictures, sounds, body sensations and internal dialog. It seems to be mainly situated in and around the head.

The **Unconscious Mind/subconscious Mind** serves as a personal library; it stores a vast amount of information about you, your beliefs, memories and values relating to your body and the history of your life. This mind runs all your habits. It is in charge of all the things that you are able to perform automatically. It is situated inside and around the body.

Personally, I believe that the signal to leave the army came from the Creative Mind and went to the Conscious Mind via the Subconscious Mind.

SECTION 1
BELIEFS

The old shamans claimed that, – "The world is what you think it is". If that is true, it becomes much easier to follow the headline from step 1: Take responsibility for your life. This means that your life – what you experience through your sensory system – is a result of your inner world or internal map. This chapter is about how you can get to know more about this inner world. The more you know about your inner world, the better you will understand what is possible for you. You will gain clarity about the aspects you may want to adjust in order to achieve the life you want. Let's start with looking into the belief system.

I have met clients who believed that they did not deserve to have success in life. Their belief confirmed itself and they were not successful.

I have met clients who believed that life is an adventure and because of this, they have found ways to have this confirmed.

Some clients believe that they were born poor and are going to remain poor for the rest of their lives. Their minds seek ways to confirm these beliefs. In other words:

Beliefs will verify themselves! We can always find evidence for a belief that we hold!

Beliefs are our internal truth, they can support us in getting what we want or they can limit us. We simply attract everything we believe in our lives. Below are some examples of beliefs that are limiting and some examples of the supportive beliefs they could be replaced with:

	Miting beliefs	Supportive beliefs
a.	I am not good enough	I am me and I am good enough
b.	Life is a battle	What I really want comes easily to me
c.	There is no love for me	Love flows through everything in my life

| d. | I never succeed with… | Whatever I really focus on, I will succeed with |
| e. | It is easier for everybody else to… | I can create what I want in my life |

These are examples to inspire you to think of your own. Now I would like you to make your own list. Perhaps you will find yourself protesting that life has shown you that your beliefs are absolutely true. **Please remember that the function of beliefs is to verify themselves.** *or, to quote Henry Ford: "Whether you believe you can do a thing or not, you are right"!*

Exercise 1: Find the patterns/beliefs in your life

Flexible people and organizations have an advantage over less flexible! This is one of the principles and you might nod your head and say that it sounds absolutely right. And it does sound very easy, doesn't it? But the question is of course: How does one stay flexible in practise? This section contains exercises that can support you to gain greater flexibility and to expand your Model of the World. It has everything to do with your beliefs.

Our beliefs are often found in the unconscious part of our Model of the World, beyond our conscious memory so we must go exploring in order to discover them. The patterns in our life will lead us to them; behind every pattern is a kind of program, consisting of one or more beliefs.

I will now invite you to find the patterns in your life that actually prevent you from being or doing what you want. There are no right or wrong answers to the following questions. The purpose is merely to give you the opportunity to discover your patterns. What conclusions you draw from this is, of course, your own decision.

Employment

How are things in the area of employment? What do you think about your own skills? Do you think that you are very skilled – or not? (belief)

Do you have an easy relationship with your colleagues or

do you keep your distance and think that some of them are difficult to be around? What about managers – do they listen to you or do you always need to push hard to get your ideas heard? What do you think about other people? (belief)

Do you believe in yourself when you go to negotiate your salary or do you hear a really insecure inner voice that tells you it's no use, you don't deserve a higher salary? (belief)

Do you have success in your job or must you always fight for your results?

(belief about one or the other)

Parents

You can work on these issues regardless of whether your parents are still alive or not. Our relationship with our parents influences our relationships with other people for life, so we include it here.

Is/was it natural for you to visit your parents or would/did you prefer to avoid it? What is/was it you want/wanted to avoid? Why? (*belief*)

Can /could you have a casual conversation with your parents or do/did you often get a negative feeling in your body during a conversation with them? What is it about? (*belief*)

Do/did you have an especially difficult relationship with one of your parents? What is it that makes/made it difficult? (*belief*)

Personal relationships

Do you have long lasting personal relationships or are you always on your way to the next one? What do you think about love? (belief)

Can you trust your loved one or do you have an inner voice that warns you? What does it say? (*belief*)

Can you tolerate your loved one's 'bad habits' or do you get annoyed by them? What is that about? (*belief*)

Do you like to keep yourself looking good for your loved one or are you indifferent? What is that about? (*belief*).

Can you be honest with your loved one or do you keep parts of your life secret? What is the reason for that? (*belief*)

Do you think it is easy to be with friends (one or more) or do you mostly keep to yourself? Do you feel secure in relationships with others or are you always wary of their reaction? What do you think about other people in relation to you? (*belief*)

Body & Health

Do you like your body or do you think it is ugly? What do you think about your own body? (*belief*)

Does the energy float freely in your body or do you have many tensions? What is that about? (*belief*)

Do you have frequent stomach aches, headaches or are you slightly stressed? What causes that? What do you think about time for yourself, about duty? (*belief*)

Are you physically active and keep yourself fit or are you indifferent? What do you think about staying fit? (*belief*)

Are you aware of the quality of the foods you choose or do you just buy the cheapest possible? Do you use food as consolation or encouragement? What do you think about food? (*belief*)

Economy

Do you think there is plenty for you or have you always experienced the opposite? (*belief*) Do you ask for what you think you are worth in your work or do you think you can't do that? (*belief*)

Do you give to others of your abundance, or do you think that they must get by on their own? (*belief*)

Do you save a lot in order to have financial security or do you think you will always be able to get by? What do you really believe about money?

(*belief*)

I suggest that you answer the questions as honestly as possible.

When you have written down all the answers – the beliefs – run through the list and evaluate whether those beliefs are supporting you or limiting you in getting what you want in life. Make a list of limiting beliefs for later use.

Section 2
Values – Your personal motivators

An important part of the Model of the World is the area of personal values. Values run our lives; they are the emotional motivators behind what we do. They make us get up every morning to go to work, they can make us drive our elderly neighbour to the supermarket for supplies or take 5 noisy boys to play in a football match. Why do we do such things even when they are sometimes inconvenient? The answer is because it gives us something – there is a strong personal value, or passion, behind the action. Values are characterised by being connected to emotions; they feel important to us. The stronger the emotion, the more passionate we are. Powerful emotions and passions create an enormous amount of motivation inside us.

The following section on values aims to guide you through a value clarification process. This will be the basis for your later work on creating the life you want.

When we work with personal values, we can work in general or we can split them into areas of life such as work, relationships, housing, family, body and health or personal development. Values exist in a kind of hierarchy, with those that are most important to us at the top. It is therefore very useful to know our most important values because they are the biggest motivators for us.

Areas of life can be:

- Work
- Relationships
- Family and friends
- Housing
- Body & Health
- Personal development

Exercise 2: Find the Values

Find a pen and paper and make sure you are not interrupted for the next 15 minutes. Make yourself comfortable. Light a candle, put on some stimulating music or do whatever makes you feel good. Choose an area of life which you feel is important for you right now. Perhaps you will choose one that you are experiencing some problems with at the moment. Then start asking yourself:

"*What is really important to me?*"

"*What does... (something)... really mean to me?*"

"*What do I want to do? What will it give me to do that?*"

Write down your answers. They are your values in this area of life.

Values are often expressed as words or short phrases. You find your values by simply asking inside yourself for them. You continue on as long as you can keep coming up with answers and by the end you will have your list of values. For some people the list contains perhaps only 5 values and for some it will be 25. There are no rules for that.

Exercise 3: Make a spontaneous prioritization of values

Take a look at your list and start to prioritize them in order of importance. Ask which one is the most important and make it number 1. Run through the whole list in this way. It is very useful to know the three most important values within each life area, as they provide a lot of motivation. Similarly, it can cause great frustration and dissatisfaction if your most important values are not being met in your life. As you do this exercise, you may find that a shift of values happens if you discover an area that requires some changes.

Exercise 4: Make a further prioritization of values

The next step is to make sure that your list is correct and you have the values listed in order of importance. This can be done by using the process below. You simply ask:

"What is most important, this value (1) or this value (2)"?

Then you ask "What is most important, this value (1) or this value (3)"?

You continue to compare all the values to each other until you are sure you have found your most important value. Call that value number 1.

Then you take value 1 and ask:

"If you already have this value (1), what is the next most important, value (2) or value (3)"?

You continue like this until the whole hierarchy of values has been worked through.

Exercise 5: How can you get your values met?

By doing this value clarification process, you make your inner motivation clear within this area of your life, as it stands at this moment. Based on this knowledge and motivation, you can start to create your goals – the plans for how you can live congruently with your inner motivation (your values). Goals are merely your practical plans for how to turn your values into reality. We will work with goal-setting in chapter 6. For now, you can start to reflect on how well your values are being met at the moment and whether it is time to make some changes in this area of your life.

How often should you work on your values?

There will be time when your values are quite stable. There will be other times when your values are more or less in constant change - often becoming evident through feelings of frustration. It can happen because of major changes in your life; you get divorced; you lose a lot of money; you get fired from your job etc., or it can arise out of a desire for change. When there are constant changes happening, it can be useful to periodically check your values by conduction value clarification process. This makes it easier for you to understand yourself and what is going on in your life at that moment.

Exercise 6: Working with another person to elicit values

Working with a friend can make it even easier for you to find your values.

2 persons, A and B.

1. A assists B to find his/hers values in his chosen area of life.

A asks B : What is important to you in the area of _____? (work, health etc.)

other questions could be:

- What must be present in _____ (specify a life area) for you to thrive?
- What can you not be without in the area of _____?
- Think of an experience you have had which was really valuable for you (within the chosen area, e.g. work) – what was important about that experience?

2. A assists B to prioritize the values / find the value hierarchy

Prioritizing can be done in two ways:

a) A asks B to do a spontaneous prioritization by asking:

- Please prioritize these values so that the most important is no. 1, the second most important is no. 2 etc. or,
- Which is the most important value? or,
- Which stands out the most?

b) A asks B to be more meticulous with his prioritizing, comparing the values by asking:

- Which is most important, this value or that value?
- If you already have this value (no.1) which is the next most important – this one, or that one?

When this has been done, A asks B to rewrite the list of values in priority order.

SECTION 3
YOUR COMMUNICATION

We now understand that whenever we say and/or do something to another person, our actions will undoubtedly be deleted, generalized and distorted in the other person's Model of the World. We refer to this as *communication*. The other person will perceive our communication through their sensory system, it will pass through their filter and they will create an 'internal representation' or, in other words, they will draw a conclusion. How often does this happen? All the time! We all are dependent on each other: we get results by talking, listening, negotiating and playing with other people, and they get what they want by interacting with us. So becoming aware of how this communication takes place can be the key to success or failure. Let´s see how you can improve your results.

Communication consists of:
- Words
- Body language
- Voice

Rapport
When two people sit, engrossed in conversation, you often find that their body language and voice tone is largely similar. Maybe they lift their cups from the table at the same time, and if one of them changes his way of sitting the second follows – quite unconsciously.

We can say that when two people have good contact, they act similarly - in body language, tone, and linguistic terms. They send a subconscious signal to each other that says "we are alike" – a signal that makes both parties comfortable and confident. We say they have good rapport.

Matching
To create rapport, we can consciously match different things about the other person. For example, their body language, tone

of voice or special gestures. Matching must be discreet, and shifts must be made a little after the other person so that it is quite subtle – very obvious matching might cause the opposite effect, otherwise known as 'mismatching'.

To be even more discreet, one can do 'cross-over matching', for example, by matching another person's head movement with our hand movement, or the other person's hand movement with a similar motion with our own foot.

To create deep rapport, there are many different things one can match, such as body language, breathing, movements of body, gestures, voice pitch, speaking rate, etc. Practising this over time will make it an unconscious habit, which means that you will have good rapport with others without even having to think about it.

Next do the following 2 exercises:

Exercise 7: Observation of matching

Watch some TV interviews and notice the areas where the participants match and where they mis-match.

Exercise 8: Match the people you talk to

Consciously start matching others when you talk to them and notice the results you get.

Practise doing it as discreetly as possible.

Chunking

We can use the term *chunking* to describe the level of abstraction in communication. It can make a great deal of difference whether a person speaks in the abstract and general level or at a more specific level.

An example: Two people talk abstractly about transportation in the countryside. One thinks of his new big BMW (and finds transportation swift), whereas the other thinks of public transport (and finds transportation lengthy). If they keep it abstract, without chunking down to what mode of transportation they are talking about, they may misunderstand each other.

The example on the next page shows how to chunk up to the more abstract and chunk down to the more specific. There is also an example of how to side-chunk, i.e. find more examples at the same level of abstraction.

Chunking can be used in many contexts. In the next paragraph you can read about The Linguistic Model and learn how to get an understanding of a person's Model of the World by listening to their language. Chunking is part of this. In chapter 6 you can read about the Neurological Levels which are another way to chunk up and down, and in chapter 7 you can learn about self-hypnosis, a third way to deal with abstraction.

An example of chunking

If you start with the phrase "football match", you can chunk up, down and to the side in the following manner:

Figure 10

You can move towards a higher level of abstraction (chunk up) by asking the question: "What is this an example of?" or "What is this a part of?"

You move towards the more specific (chunk down) by asking the question:

"What specifically?" or "What is an example of this?"

Please do the following exercise youself.

Exercise 9:

Take the word car and chunk it up and down by using the above questions.

SECTION 4
THE LINGUISTIC MODEL (LM)

LM has its roots in the Meta-Model from NLP which goes all the way back to Noam Chomsky's[2] idea of the division of communication into three categories: Deletions, Generalisations and Distortions. LM is a simplified version based on the premise that the process we use to create our internal representation is also used to create our internal linguistic representation of experience.

This means that what we say during communication reveals a lot of our internal Model of the World. By simply listening to other people's language, you can gain a lot of information about their thinking. You may have noticed that some people use very unspecific language and LM can help you better understand the meaning.

We will separate the use of the model into two areas:

- Listening to others, and
- Listening to yourself.

By paying attention to the structure of language, we can learn a lot about another person's way of thinking. By listening to ourselves we start to create choices in life, "How am I speaking and what is my own structure of thinking?" Does this way of speaking support me or is it time to adjust my way of speaking by adjusting my way of thinking?"

Deletions

Let's start with looking closer at deletions. A deletion means that some information is missing. Since the language is not complete, it may be difficult to get the specific meaning out of it. We may think we understand the speaker but we can't be sure. We can ask ourselves, "Do I really understand the meaning?" Deletions are about listening for the information

---

2. Noam Chomsky, linguist, philosopher and debater – (among others) known for a naturalistic approach to the study of linguistics – who has had a strong influence on the way we think of the link between language and mind today.

that is not given. By asking for this information we can gain a better understanding.

E.g. *"There were many people"* – The speaker has a complete picture inside her mind but leaves out the details so the specific meaning is unclear.

You can ask, *"Many? How many is many for you?"* to give you a clear understanding. Using this part of the LM model, you can uncover specific parts of the speaker's Model of the World, i.e. get more information.

Some more examples:

E.g. *"She is so closed"* – There is not enough information to be sure you understand what the speaker really means. To clarify that you are thinking the same, you can ask, *"What do you mean by closed?"* or *"How/when do you experience that she is closed?"*

E.g. *"I cannot be bothered with that anymore"*.

Q: "What is it that you can't be bothered with anymore?"

E.g. *"I am so angry"*

Q: What are you so angry about?

or someone may delete who, or what, they are referring to.

E.g. *"They never talk with each other"*

Q: Who never talks with each other?

E.g. *"This is not going to work"*

Q: What is not going to work? Sometimes we delete information about whom or what we compare.

E.g. *"She is much better at Spanish"*

Q: Compared to whom / compared to what?

When people talk, they do it from different Models of the World, believing that the words and phrases they use have similar meanings for others. In daily conversation this means that we often assume that we are all talking about the same thing, when in fact we are not. Words can have multiple meanings.

E.g. *"Have you seen much of Henry lately?"*

Q: What do mean by much?

By asking, we can make sure that we are talking about the same thing, not merely speculating or assuming what the other person actually means.

E.g. *"It was a really good night, lots of things going on, and the show that Kim put on went on wheels!"*

Q: What do you mean by 'on wheels'?

Exercise 10:

Write some examples of your own.

Generalizations

The mind generalizes information – that is part of its function. This means that new information coming through the filter will be compared with information already stored in the Subconscious Mind and generalized if possible. The subconscious is lazy and won't create a new meaning if it can stick to an old one. The fact that we can generalize means that we don't need to start over every day; we can use what we have already learned. The disadvantage is that it also creates some inflexibility in the mind – it holds us to a certain experience of things. If I experience everyone who wears a certain type of glasses as a 'nerd', I will prevent myself from experiencing any new person I meet as he really is. In my Model of the World he is a nerd – he has those glasses!

Let's look at some examples:

E.g. *"I will never learn this"*. – What is the thinking here? It means that until now it has not been possible to learn this. But at any time it may be possible to gain a new perspective and learn it. If the speaker continues to say *"I will never learn this"*, he is programming himself to never learn it. How about you – do you ever use this kind of generalization? Listen to your own language over a period of time. You can challenge the generalization by asking: *"Never? Never ever?"*

E.g. *"I have to do it."* – What is the thinking here? The speaker can't see any choices or find a way to express their need. It may be true or it may not be true. In most situations, we actually have a choice; we just haven't seen it yet. This kind of statement is motivated by consequence so it can be challenged by asking: *"What will happen if you don't?"* What about your own communication – how often do you use that kind of language? E.g. *"It is harmful for children to watch TV."* – What is the thinking? This generalization is based on unwritten rules; there is no source mentioned in the speaker´s statement. Is it based on scientific research? We don't know – there is no reference. How often do you use that kind of generalization? Try listening to your own language for a while to find out. If you want to challenge it you can ask, *"According to whom?"*

Other examples:

"I can never complete anything." – This is where an earlier experience has been generalized to be true in all similar situations. A challenge could be: *"Have you never, ever completed anything?"*

"All women are preoccupied with their looks." – Challenge: *"Have you ever met one woman who was not preoccupied with her looks?"*

This kind of statement often stems from a specific event where the speaker decided this view of her/himself or others.

"I ought to be more careful." – This is another example of a lack of choice inside the speaker's mind. The challenge could be: *"What do you think will happen if you are not?"*

Here is another one concerned with consequence, *"I can't just ask her."* – You can counter this with, *"What keeps you from doing it? What would happen if you did?"*

The above generalizations tell us that the speaker does not perceive his capability to have any influence. However, it is often just the speaker's *experience* that is limiting, not his capabilities.

By being challenged with questions such as those above, the speaker can become aware of the limitations in their thoughts and can reflect upon how functional this way of thinking is for them.

Spend some time paying attention to your own generalizations and discover how they actually limit your thinking and flexibility. As you notice them, use the challenge questions on yourself and notice how, over time, your own thinking and options are expanded.

Distortions

In chapter one, we discussed how the mind distorts things in order to fit the Model of the World. We may now be able to see how distortions contribute to maintaining our problems in life. Distortion means that **we interpret reality and change it so it fits our Model of the World,** and this is how our beliefs are confirmed. This is, of course, beneficial with positive beliefs (for instance: *"He smiles, so he thinks I am good!"*) but it can be worth challenging the limiting ones, such as those mentioned in the examples below.

When someone states what another person is thinking without having asked them, we call it 'mind reading'. If we believe we already know what other people think and feel, we limit ourselves.

For example:

"The others think I'm stupid, so I keep my mouth shut." – This is pure mind reading and can be challenged in this way, "How do you know that the others think you're stupid"? Any mind reading, in self or others, can be countered with a *"How do you know...?"* question to raise awareness of it.

E.g. *"He doesn't like me"* can be challenged by asking, *"What makes you think that"*?

As we learned in the last chapter, the first step in Self-coaching is: *take responsibility for everything in your life.* Become the cause of your life, not the effect. Many people experience their emotions as being **caused by** the actions of other people or a specific event. In other words, they are feeling good or bad because something or someone has affected them. This can show up in personal relationships, e.g. *"you* **make me** *sad"*, or it can have more abstract associations such as *"the tax system has ruined me"* (**made me** poor). In either case, we take on the role of victim – trying to get the other person or the system to change in order for us to feel better.

When a person expresses that s/he has specific feelings because of the actions of someone else or because of other external causes, we call it "cause-effect". We recognize this category by the words **makes me** or **causes me** (possibly implicit in the phrase). We can raise the awareness of the speaker to the fact that there isn't necessarily a connection between what the other person does (the cause) and their reactions to that (the effect). In this way, the speaker is enabled to take responsibility for his/her own feelings and inner states, freeing them from being the victim.

This also applies to the self. We can pay attention to our own words and notice when we blame an external cause for something. By doing this we create the opportunity to choose to reclaim the power.

E.g. *"Their laughter drives me insane"* can be challenged by, *"What makes you react this way?"*

With this question, the attention of the speaker is directed away from the other person and toward their own inner experiences. This enables them to do something about the problem, because they now become the cause instead of the effect.

You might also raise the speaker's awareness to the possibility of a pattern, where the reaction does not necessarily have anything to do with the other person.

E.g. *"She makes me feel foolish"* can be met with *"Can you think of other situations where you get the same feeling?"*

or you can go directly to exploring the choices:

E.g. *"I get so tired, he speaks so much!"* – You can ask, *"What choices do you have in this situation?"*

Take time to analyze some examples from your past to find out how often you have made others the cause of what happens in your life. Start to pay attention to your language from now on.

Exercise 11:

Think back through your history and write down the most common generalizations and distortions you use.

SECTION 5
THE AUTOPILOT – OUR UNCONSCIOUS HABITS/
STRATEGIES

We all have habits. We may know some of our own and certainly we have noticed that of others – especially those we don´t like. Some people practically live their lives without any awareness of their habits and strategies; they bother others with their habits without knowing it. This is sometimes referred to as "sleeping while awake".

Our habits are stored in the unconscious mind, rather like a set of programs, similar to the programs within a computer. Things that happen to us cause certain 'programmed' reactions. For example, you hear the voice of your loved one and it creates a good feeling or you see a beautiful sunrise and feel very peaceful.

This is so natural for us that we don't really think about how it happens. However, inside the unconscious mind a lot of things are taking place and this section is about how we can create consciousness about those deep "programs" and how we can adjust those which are now unhelpful for us.

We spend roughly the first seven years of life creating and anchoring most of our habits – or strategies – by modelling those around us; parents, siblings, extended family, teachers etc. Those strategies or programs remain with us, often without question as to whether they are still suitable for us. Some may seem a little 'childish' once we have matured to adulthood, for example, imagine that you hold a position within a company and whenever the manager walks toward your desk, you feel uncomfortable – as if you are being checked up on. Of course, this would be unpleasant for you and would not foster a collaborative relationship with the manager. It could be that you are having an unconscious reaction (from an internal program) that you can't explain, linked to something that happened in your early years.

Once the mind develops a certain pattern, it repeats itself over and over again without any conscious thought. It is advantageous that we can leave the unconscious mind to take care of the routine work so that we do not have to concentrate, for instance, tie shoelaces or fasten buttons. As a result, the conscious mind is kept free for more interesting activities. However, when the mind repeats a habit or strategy that is unpleasant or even limiting for us, it becomes more of a problem. That's when we discover that we are not consciously in control because unconscious strategies have taken over: our internal 'autopilot' is guiding us.

We all have such an internal autopilot which guides us in everyday tasks. For example, most people who habitually drive a car can do it without thinking specifically about the method. Even more commonplace is the process of how you raise your body from a chair – it is so automatic that you can do it without even wasting a thought on it, your body just knows how.

So, how do you do it? Try this as an experiment. Position yourself in a chair and when you are comfortable slowly begin to rise to your feet. Pay attention to all the steps your body runs through to do it. What is the first step? Is it leaning forward? What is the next step? We call such a series of steps a 'strategy'. **A strategy is a certain sequence of actions which produce the same result each time** – in this case, getting up from a chair.

Whether we deem a strategy suitable or not depends on the structure of the steps we go through, i.e. whether we are satisfied with the process and outcome. A person who has difficulty motivating himself to do the washing up may berate himself: *"You should… it's really bad that you…"*, and perhaps holds an internal representation of the job as a big, dark, unpleasant task. A more suitable strategy would be to see the cleared kitchen table and feel the joy of having finished the work.

In this section, we will look at what strategies consist of and how you can consciously create the best motivational and decision strategies.

The overall elements in a strategy are:
Goal – Evidence – Action – Evaluation

Example: Strategy for getting up in the morning:
Goal: Get out of bed in the morning Evidence:
Feeling the feet on the floor Action:
Moving the body out of bed Evaluation:
I check that my desired evidence is consistent with reality (feet on the floor).

The action part consists of a sequence of components or steps that will determine whether I reach my goal or not.
For instance, these action steps could be:

Step 1: I wake up, feeling my body in the bed

Step 2: I open my eyes and look around the room

Step 3: I make inner pictures of appealing circumstances to come during the day

Step 4: I think to myself: "Hmm – let me get out of bed!"

Step 5: I move the muscles in my body that get me out of bed
> These steps are made from components such as inner pictures, sounds, words and body sensations.

Please do the following exercise.

Exercise 12:

Next time you perform an everyday act such as making a sandwich or a cup of coffee, think about the steps that are part of this action. What is going on inside you (your thoughts)? What steps take place externally?

Have paper and pen ready, and write down some of the steps, for instance:

• I see the contents of the fridge

• I see a cheese sandwich in my mind's eye

- I imagine tasting the sandwich
- I feel the bread in my hand while cutting a slice... etc.

Changing a strategy

Once we have uncovered one of our inadequate strategies, we can change the steps in the action part to create a more effective strategy which will give us a better outcome.

It is pretty simple; we have an inadequate strategy, we study this to find the steps and then we change the one or more steps in the action to get a better process or result.

An example:

D has a strategy for making herself feel insecure when she most needs to feel secure.

Goal: Feel secure Evidence:

Making a decision that feels right Action:

Step 1: D faces a choice

Step 2: D says to herself "I wonder what's the right decision?"

Step 3: D voices one of the choices in a hesitant tone

Step 4: D thinks: "oh, that's probably wrong" and feels insecure.

Step 5: D says aloud the opposite choice

Step 6: D sees that others around her look confused and hears them ask her whether she means one or the other

Step7: D then says to herself: "Stupid me" and feels uncomfortable.

Evaluation: Feels insecure and uncomfortable.

This is certainly an inadequate strategy because it does not lead to the desired goal. A modification of this strategy could be made at step 2 where D could instead say to herself: "I take my time to feel what seems right for me". This would change the rest of the strategy:

Step 1: D faces a choice

Step 2: D says to herself: "I take my time to feel what seems right for me."

Step 3: D makes some internal pictures of the different options and makes a decision based on how those affect her.

Step 4: D voices her choice.

Evaluation: Feels secure, has made a decision that feels right.

The most important part of adjusting an inadequate strategy is to discover the internal steps – often the first step in a strategy is the appearance of an image in the mind or the sound of an inner voice and then the rest of the steps follow on from that.

Practising the new strategy

Once we have analysed the old strategy and replaced one of the steps with a new action, we need to repeat the new strategy a number of times until the unconscious mind has installed and anchored it as a program.

A simple way to do this is by walking the steps. Going back to the example above, D positions herself at a point on the floor and faces her choice.

- D physically moves one step forward and says to herself: "I take my time to feel what seems right for me".

- D takes another step forward and makes some internal pictures of the different options.

- D moves one more step forward and evaluates those options one by one.

- D takes another step forward, senses which one will work best and chooses that.

- D continues to anchor this procedure by walking it again at least three times.

It is always preferable to have all three representational systems – visual, auditory and kinaesthetic – included in the procedure. Initially, the new strategy can be evaluated for how well it functions and thereafter anchored again and again until it works unconsciously.

Decision strategies

On any ordinary day, we make a long series of decisions about large and small things – what will I have for lunch? Should I do this job first? Shall I say it now or later? For some people it is easy to make decisions while for others it takes time. Naturally, how easy it is also depends on the scale and consequences of the decision. Nevertheless, it has been identified that certain components recur in good decision making strategies and poor decision strategies can lead to unnecessary problems. A good decision strategy will prevent many problems!

A decision strategy normally works best if it contains the following elements:

- Visual construction of different options
- Consciousness about criteria for the choice
- Inclusion of all representational systems

Visual construction of different options

Some people use either visually remembered situations or no pictures in their decision strategy. However, it is important to have access to visual options to create new choices.

Consciousness about criteria for the choice

In a good decision strategy, one considers all criteria at once, prioritizing so that the biggest emphasis is put on the most important aspect. If, for example one goes to buy a new stereo, it is important to know that the criteria are good sound, good design and reasonable price. A good strategy will involve all criteria at the same time with awareness of the most and least important so that the minor points can be let go of if necessary. A poor strategy would be where one was unaware of the criteria, running from shop to shop without being able to decide, or where one sets up criteria that are unattainable.

All representational systems included

In a good decision strategy, the visual, auditory and kinaesthetic impressions are included. In a poor strategy, one or more impressions may be missing, for example, only the visual impression of the new stereo is considered, forgetting that the sound is also important. Another problem may be that one does not trust one's own senses, preferring to trust what others say or do. This can create internal confusion and indecision. should I rely on myself or others? Please do the following exercise.

Exercise 13:

Imagine that you are going to buy something new for your home. Go through the elements in the above process, and notice if there is anything you need to change in your decision strategy.

Motivational strategies – good self-management

Being good at self-management presupposes that one is good at having an overview, prioritizing, making decisions – and not least, motivating oneself!

A good motivational strategy normally includes some important components:

- **A pleasant inner voice:** "It'll be fun once I get started" which leads to

- **A constructed picture of the finished job and / or**

- **Absorption in the process with an enjoyable feeling** – which leads to more **action**.

Ineffective motivation may be caused by:

Dictatorial inner voice

If the tone of the inner voice is accusatory and full of modal verbs (should, must, have to) then frequently this will lead to a lack of desire to do the job. Switching to an encouraging voice - inviting instead of ordering – often has a significant effect.

Overwhelming subs

Some people imagine the whole task as one big mass piling up in front of them. This makes most people feel reluctant to start or depressed and stressed about the workload. To overcome this, start by changing the subs i.e. make the inner picture smaller and push it further away. Then begin splitting it into partial goals, or steps. Continue to break it down into smaller steps until the first step seems very easy to accomplish.

Away-from motivation

Away-from motivation means that we are trying to motivate ourselves by imagining negative consequences of not doing the task - we are motivated by moving away from the consequences. Such a motivation may work sometimes to get the work started, but it creates an unpleasant feeling and if it is not replaced by toward – motivation, the work will feel very heavy.

Visual construction of doing the job instead of it being finished.

If you have a very boring task which must be completed, it is difficult to motivate yourself to do it by thinking of the process. Thinking about the *finished* work is much more motivating. Sometimes it can be even more motivating to go a step further and think about what it will give you to have the work finished, i.e. the value of it, or the ' goal behind the goal.'

Please do the following exercise.

Exercise 14: Lack of Motivation

Think of a task that you have postponed for a long time. Explore your inner representation of the task:

- Visually
- Auditory
- Kinaesthetically

Now construct a picture of how it will look when you have finished it.

SECTION 6
YOUR SPECIAL GIFT!

Some people claim that we are all here for a reason and that we all have something to offer the world. I think this is right, and it can be delightful to discover the special gift that we bring to the world.

Exercise 15:

Take some paper and begin to reflect on what you are very good at. What do you always succeed at doing? In what areas do you think yourself talented? From time to time, review this list and do the exercise again until you get the sense that you know your special gifts and they will begin to play a bigger part in your life.

CHAPTER 3

EXPLORE THE PRESENT

....

You may have access to the Video and Audio pack which can be bought as supplement to the Self-coaching book. In that case I would recommend this for chapter 3:

Video: Balancing positions. The Walt Disney Model

Audio: Balancing positions. Quiet Mind 2

....

Your time is limited so don't waste it living someone else's life. Don't be trapped by dogma – which is living with the results of other people's thinking. Don't let the noise of others' opinions drown out your own inner voice. And most important, have the courage to follow your heart and intuition.

—Steve Jobs

Some years ago, I was leading an Akasha Healing Training on the Islands of Hawaii. Helene and I had taken a group from Europe to explore the particularly special energy there. our base was in Hilo, near the active volcano on the Big Island. Then we went to Kauai, The Garden Island – which flourishes so well because of the high annual rainfall. This also means it is often covered in clouds.

On the last day of the training, we went to Polihale Beach on the northwest coast. It was a special day with a great feeling of expectation in the air, as there always is on the Akasha Trainings. It really felt like something extraordinary was about to happen. When we arrived at Polihale Beach in the late afternoon, the sky was perfectly clear and the sun was shining. Helene and I gave instructions for the students to position themselves for the evening: they were to find a place and sit alone in meditation for a number of hours, simply being totally present with all senses activated.

From our spot in the dunes, we watched the sunset and listened to the sound of the 12 foot waves crashing onto the shore; it was quite magical.

Gradually, Sunlight started to fade away and the stars started to become more visible. Within an hour, the whole sky was covered with stars. Over the next two hours, we felt as if the stars were descending down to us and all we needed to do was stretch arms to touch them. Time stopped and we became one with the stars. Everyone shared this feeling of being totally present – no thoughts, no internal dialogue – with the whole sensory system activated to absorb as much of the experience as possible. It truly was a breathtaking event for all of us.

This chapter is about being present in the Now. It describes how to be totally present to more of life's events – similar to that experienced by the group in Hawaii. When we are totally present we are able to experience life fully. I am sure you have encountered those kinds of moments and perhaps you wonder what prevents you from always having that level of experience. In fact, it is the mind that prevents it. The mind is working all the time, producing images, sounds, body sensations and internal dialogue. Indeed, most of us walk around in a kind of 'cloud of thoughts' and that's where we put our awareness. We have done it for so long that we don't really believe it can be any different. We think it's natural and that life needs to be that way.

Some people place a lot of their attention in the future; they love their dreams and take every opportunity to move towards them. They like to spend time thinking about how their life could become. Other people pay a lot of attention to the past, thinking back to former situations and repeatedly analyzing how they could have done things differently. They may even blame themselves for things that didn't go well. However, some people actually live in the present with little interest in visions or past experience.

In fact, life unfolds from moment to moment and we can be totally present to each of those, allowing us to experience the full joy of life.

It is true that we make new decisions in the Present, but if the Conscious Mind does not give 'new instruction' to the unconscious Mind, it will simply recreate the past. This is what we are doing most of the time – recreating our past. Our numerous habits are repeated without even thinking about it. In some circles, this is referred to as 'being asleep' and I guess this could be a good description for a life where the same things take place over and over again.

So, is that wrong? Not at all – it's a very stable way of life. Yet, sooner or later, people come to a point in their lives where they are meant to experience something totally different – something that may have been 'encoded' into their timeline by their Higher Mind. For that reason, it will come at exactly the right time, giving us the chance to really learn something new. This is the moment when we are confronted with new opportunities and are offered the chance to change our life. However, we don't always see it as an 'offer'—sometimes we call it a 'disaster' because a part of our personality would rather life continued in the familiar way.

In my experience, it seems that most people get this type of opportunity at least once in their lifetime. It can be because of a divorce. That's what happened in my life. It can happen through an unforeseen career change or unemployment. For some, it comes about from a sudden or unexpected death in the family. Some of these 'offers' come in the form of a serious illness, allowing us to make some important decisions about our life. These events are not really disasters – they are more like 'wake up calls' or invitations to look inside for the deeper meaning of your life and start to live congruently with that.

We can also have dreams or visions for our life. A vision is like a lighthouse, lighting up the horizon and showing us where to go. They tell us about our future. Do you have a dream for your life? Have you ever written down your dream? If not, you may want to do it now. Please just go ahead and write it. Allow 8-10 minutes for this exercise.

Exercise 1: My Dream for my Life is...

So what about the past - what is it useful for? The past is our history; it represents our knowledge, skills and experience and creates stability in our life. It contains all that we have learned and is what we rely upon when we stand at crossroads of life with a choice to make. Some of it may require a little adjustment: limiting beliefs or internal parts that represent habits from our childhood. For example. However, I think it is important to remember that the present is the only thing that exists. We live in the Present; we make decisions and have our experiences in the Present. In my opinion, it is important to have a balance between the Past, the Present and the Future. This is what we will explore in this chapter. I suggest we start by exploring three different perspectives on reality.

SECTION 1
HOW WE EXPERIENCE REALITY.
PERCEPTUAL POSITIONS

There's a well-known phrase: *"to see things from a different perspective"*. If we take this literally, it suggests that it's possible to experience things from other perspectives - or perceptual positions – as well as through our own eyes. It has been discovered that we do indeed do that; we can see things from another's perspective or see events from the 'outside'. I have found the conscious use of this to be very beneficial.

I will refer to 3 perceptual positions: 1st, 2nd, and 3rd:

1st position is when I experience the world around me from my own perspective.

2nd position is where I experience the world from another person's perspective – 'stepping into somebody else's shoes'.

3rd position is when I experience myself and the other person(s) from outside as a 'neutral observer'.

1st position is useful for knowing what I want, what my values are and for setting boundaries.

2nd position is useful for understanding another person's Model of the World – 'to step into their shoes'.

Note: in order to be truly valuable, it's important to be able to step back into your own 'shoes' and separate yourself from the other (e.g. I don't help someone who is sad, by starting to cry mysel).

3rd position is useful for getting a neutral overview of the situation: seeing yourself and the other person from the outside. In 3rd position we only calibrate and it is a good perspective for checking rapport. This position is sometimes referred to as the 'the fly on the wall'.

Exercise 2
Please do the following exercise: Physically change positions
Think of a meeting or a conversation you have had – choose

one that did not go quite the way you wanted.

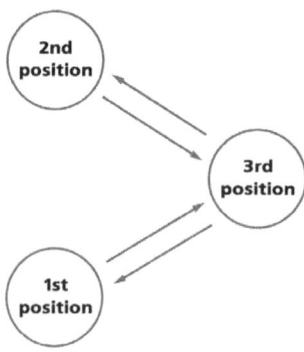

Figure 11

Place 3 chairs on the floor, and let them represent 1st, 2nd and 3rd position. or simply put 3 pieces of paper on the floor and write the positions on them.

Start in 1st position and relive the conversation – what was it like to be you in the situation?

Next, go to 3rd position. Watch and listen to the conversation from the outside as if you were a spectator. Notice the rapport between 1st and 2nd position.

Then go to 2nd position and engage from this perspective – what thoughts and feelings do you experience?

Go back to 3rd position and observe again from the outside, staying as neutral as possible.

End with the 1st position and notice whether you would choose to do something different the next time you are in a similar situation.

SECTION 2
THE WALT DISNEY MODEL

Now let's look at another technique: The Walt Disney Model. It was created by the American NLP trainer Robert Dilts who studied a series of successful people to find the basis for their success. One of those was Walt Disney, who possessed the ability to not only get ideas but to put them into practice. From this study, Robert Dilts discovered a process which requires to 'divide our personality into three aspects', namely:

The Dreamer (The future)
The Realist (The Present)
The Critic (The Past)

The Dreamer is the part of the personality that is creative. It is visionary; it creates ideas and presents them to the mind's eye. The Dreamer thinks big and would suggest that everything is possible. The Dreamer represents the Future.

The Realist is the part of the personality that tranforms the dreams into something more practical. The Realist thinks in goals, targets, time and resources and it acts to find the best plan to bring the dream into reality. The realist represents the Present.

The Critic is responsible for evaluation; for finding all the weak parts of the plan. It asks the critical questions – with the purpose of making a plan that will really work and create success. The Critic represents the Past.

Some people have a large Dreamer and a small Realist. For them, everything is possible but nothing comes of it. It all remains as dreams that never come true. These people are great at creating ideas.

Others have a strong inner Realist. These people are preoccupied with the planning process; bringing things into life and overshadows everything else. Whether the basis for the plan is really creative is not so important to them. They are good organizers.

Then, there are those with a large inner Critic. They have a great capacity to ask critical questions because they can always predict the problems in a new idea. They can predict so many difficulties with the realization of the idea that it may seem better to shelf it right away! They are good for spotting the weak parts of the plan.

It is clear that a balance between these three parts of the personality is important in any process. Robert Dilts developed a model which can be used by anyone to increase their inner balance in this area.

One of the discovered facts is that every body part has its own body language (as you remember from chapter 1, inner state and physiology influence each other so when we change physiology we also change inner state).

Below, you can see the body language which is, for most people, naturally linked to the three states:

DREAMER	REALIST	CRITIC
Head and eyes up.	Head and eyes straight ahead	Eyes down. Head down and tilted
Body posture relaxed and symmetrical.	Body posture symmetrical and centred.	Body posture a-symmetrical

You can try the 3 states by doing the following exercise 3:

1. **Take three pieces of paper a**nd write 'Dreamer', 'Planner' and 'Critic' on them. Then put them on the floor with a good distance between them.

| Dreamer | Realist | Critic |

Figure 12

2. **Step into the Dreamer position** and think of a time when you had a lot of ideas - a time when the ideas just poured out. Raise your head so you look slightly upwards and lift your hands as shown in the drawing above. Stand in a relaxed and balanced posture. See your ideas or dreams as a large picture in your mind's eye. Sense the special feeling associated with having easy access to ideas.

3. **Step into the Realist position** and think of a time when you found it really easy to make a plan. Find a specific event. Imagine you are planning something step by step that will help you achieving your goal. Totally Associate and make your body posture symmetrical and centred. Remember a time when it was easy for you to get all the 'pieces of the puzzle' to fall into place.

4. **Step into the Critic** and think of a specific event where you were good at asking critical questions, one where you could easily see the weak elements in the plan. Stand with your eyes slightly downward, maybe tilt your head a little. This posture should be more asymmetric than the others, perhaps with one hand on the chin etc.

5. **Step out again** and think about how you have used these three parts of yourself up until now and which of them you could develop further.

6. **Now take an idea** or a problem and make an image of it in your mind. Move around in the Walt Disney model and remember to associate into the corresponding body positions.

Bring your idea or problem first to the Dreamer position and work on it from this perspective where 'everything is possible'. Then move into the Realist and create a timeline for the realization of the idea or solution. Next, step into the Critic and evaluate it, finding the weak aspects of the plan. Bring those weak parts or questions back to the Dreamer and find solutions to them. Move to the Realist and adjust the plan. Evaluate the adjusted plan in the Critic position and continue like this for a while. Take as long as you need to fully explore the method and gain an appreciation for the powerful consequences of this process – not least is the balance of your perception between future, present and past.

I suggest you do this exercise a number of times with different ideas or problems. The effect may be that you create more balance between future, present and past *in your personality.*

I suggest you also pay attention to the subs you find in the three different positions and notice the differences when you move from the dreamer to the realist and further to the critic.

SECTION 3
INCREASING PRESENCE IN THE NOW!

Let's go back to the idea of being totally present in the Now. Think of three events from your past where you had the experience of being totally present with whole sensory system activated. Perhaps you could choose one each from your childhood, teenage years and adulthood.

Exercise 4:

Figure 13

Step 1: Create a Timeline on the floor.

Step 2: Visualize yourself in event 1 (the first of the 3 events) and associate into yourself. Totally immerse yourself and feel what it is like to be so present in the Now. Check if it is possible to make the experience even better by adjusting some subs to increase the feeling of presence: color, light, sharpness, 2 or 3 dimensional etc. Anchor the experience by touching yourself somewhere on the body. Stay there for a while, fully engaged with the feeling of presence.

Step 3: Bring this feeling of presence forward into event 2 and associate in to that experience. Have the presence from events 1 and 2 merge together and anchor it.

Step 4: Bring the feeling forward into event 3 and do the same.

Step 5: Bring the whole cumulative experience of being present into the Present and anchor it. Stay there for a while and enjoy the state of presence.

Step 6: Generalize this into the future by walking into at least three future events. Each time, fully associate into the feeling of being totally present (you may even thank your unconscious Mind for the experience) and stay there for a while to allow your unconscious Mind to learn that this is what you want for the future.

Step 7: Repeat the anchoring process into the Future a few times. And on the final one, you can continue in your future until are a wise old man/woman and look back from there. Notice how your life expanded after you decided to live with more presence in your life experiences.

Let's continue with a number of exercises to practise being present in the Now.

Exercise 5: Peripheral Vision

Find something specific to focus on, for example, a mark on the wall. Start to focus your attention on that spot: concentrate and keep focusing until you feel as if 'you have become one' with it. Now have your peripheral vision gradually move out to both sides while you continue to focus on the spot. Allow your peripheral vision to move all the way to 180 degrees and notice that your awareness increases and, as it does, your internal dialogue stops. Continue this practice for at least 5 minutes. Training yourself to use your peripheral vision to the point where it becomes an unconscious habit will expand your ability to absorb more and more information into your mind in the present. I recommend you train your peripheral vision every day until it feels like a natural way for you to live.

Exercise 6: Pay full Attention

Imagine that you are a four month old infant and associate into that feeling. Now pick up something nearby, a pen or something similar, and look at it with the curiosity of that child. Turn the object around in your hands and look at all the details. You might even bite it. Allow yourself to move into the state of exploring something totally new in your life. Pay attention to how that is for you and from now on, let that state be part of your life as often as possible.

Exercise 7: Breathing

Sit in a chair or stand up. Begin to observe your breathing. Allow your attention to follow the air as it moves in and out of your lungs. Keep focused on the process and breathe as deeply as possible. Notice how your chest moves. Count 20 deep breaths and be watchful for any small movements or reactions in your body. Become aware of how this also creates greater relaxation.

Exercise 8: Sit or stand while you do this exercise. Inhale deeply through your nose and then exhale through your mouth, making a "Haaaaa" sound as the air leaves your body. Make your exhalation longer than the inhalation. Continue as long as you like, breathing slowly and ensuring you do not get dizzy.

If dizziness does occur, simply slow down your breathing. Notice how this kind of breathing increases your presence and awareness. At the same time, it increases the energy in your body. Use it from time to time when you need extra energy.

Exercise 9: Pay full Attention

Count slowly from 1 to 10, giving it your complete undivided attention. When your mind drifts off, go back to 1 and start again. Continue until you are able to count to 10 with your full attention.

Exercise 10: Find somewhere to sit – in a room or perhaps a hotel lobby. Move your awareness to your peripheral vision and stay in that state. Now, slowly move your head and pay attention to everything you perceive. Notice all the small details: things, colors, sizes, movements etc. Be aware of sounds: from which direction, volume, stereo or mono etc. Simply pay attention to everything you notice without drawing any conclusions.

Exercise 11: Looking into Someone's Eyes

Sit close to someone and face them. Begin by looking into their eyes. You can either look in one eye or both of them if you can do that. Engage your peripheral vision while you continue to focus into the other person's eyes. As you concentrate, pay attention to what happens. Do the exercise for at least five minutes then you can talk about it.

Exercise 12: Meditation

Focus on something in the room and then move into peripheral vision. Continue focussing and empty your mind. Shift the attention towards the back of your head, as if you are watching your brain from behind. Whenever something comes up – a picture, sound, body sensation etc. – just notice it and let it go. Remain in this state of emptiness for at least 10 minutes. Do it every day, extending the time when it feels right. You can do this exercise with your eyes closed or open whatever is most comfortable for you.

Exercise 13: Paying full Attention while Walking

Start walking around in a room or outside in nature. Move into peripheral vision and pay full attention to everything you notice while walking. Walk slowly to begin with then gradually increase the speed.

Exercise 14: Pay full Attention while Walking

Do the same exercise as no. 13, but this time walk in a circle. Make it as big as feels comfortable. Notice how it is to just walk the circle, full of awareness and without any purpose.

SECTION 4
ALIGNING PERCEPTUAL POSITIONS

In the 1990's, the American NLP Trainer Connirae Andreas became aware that many people have difficulty separating the three positions – they have a mixture of 1st and 2nd, or of 1st and 3rd in their perception. She developed the technique outlined below to bring this into balance. The purpose of the technique is to create clear separation between the positions and, by doing this, create an adjustment in the filter which changes the perception of other people. This makes it easier to handle conversations which have been difficult so far.

This technique was developed by studying what characterizes a pure 1st position and a pure 3rd position in people who are naturally skilled at this.

The aim is to align the perception in such a way that when you are in 1st position, talking to someone else, you can:

- Look through your own eyes
- Hear the sound of the other person's voice with both your ears
- Have internal dialogue in the throat area that expresses, "I need, I feel…"
- Be in touch with yourself – and only your own – emotions.

And when you are in 3rd position you can:

- Watch two people talking with both your eyes (both people are the same size)
- Listen the sound of each voices in each of your ears (same volume)
- Be in a neutral state

Let's look at how to do that.

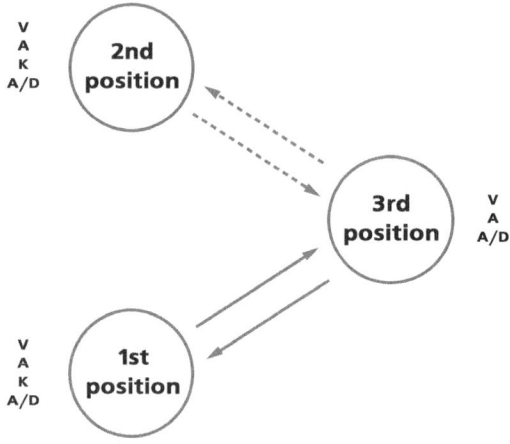

Figure 14

Exercise 15: The Balancing Technique

Step 1: Exploration of 1st position

Think of a person with whom you find communication difficult. Sit on a chair and visualize that person sitting in front of you. (It is also possible to do this process while standing).

Is the person natural sized or does he/her seems larger or smaller than normal? Notice whether you see her through your eyes or if the information comes into you somewhere else in your body.

Next, have the person talk to you in your imagination. Notice if you hear the voice in both ears or if the sound enters your body somewhere else.

If there is an internal dialogue (talking to yourself) about him/her – where does this dialogue take place: in your throat or somewhere else? What else do you notice?

Step 2: Exploration and alignment (3rd position)

Move to 3rd position. You can sit in a 3rd chair or you can stand. See both of you (your own body as well as the other person) from 3rd position. Check if you are emotionally neutral, if not, increase the distance between yourself and the two people you are 'observing' and send the emotions back to whom they belong. Once neutral, you can observe the same things as you did from 1st position, but this time, you make adjustments so that:

- You see yourself and the other in natural size.
- You perceive them only through your eyes, nowhere else.
- You hear their conversation in both your ears.

Step 3: Aligning of 1st position

Bring those adjustments back to 1st position. Sit down on the chair in 1st position and see the person in natural size and through both your eyes.

Have him/her talk to you and hear the voice in both your ears.

Have an internal dialogue about him/her and confirm that it takes place in the throat area.

Finally, you can check to see that you have a more neutral feeling about that person now.

If this is ok, go to future pace (step 5). If not, continue with step 4:

Step 4: 2nd position via 3rd position

Go back to 3rd position and make adjustments here again where necessary – visual, auditory, internal dialogue – then move to 2nd position. Sit down and associate into the other person, as if you were looking out of his/her eyes. Now start to gather information from this perspective.

Do you see yourself in natural size and with both eyes? Do you hear your own voice in both ears? Can you talk about yourself from the throat area? What kind of feelings does this person have when looking at/talking to you? What is it that goes wrong in the communication between the two of you? What does this person think about you?

Then go back to 3rd position and align one more time; adjusting to natural size, observing through your eyes, hearing their talk in both your ears and moving your internal dialogue to the area of your throat. Remember there should be no kinesthetic experience.

Step 5: 1st position: future pace

Go to 1st position and align again; see the other at natural size and through both your eyes, hear his/her voice in both ears, have internal dialogue taking place in the throat, and feel that you now have a more neutral feeling about this person.

Future pace this by imagining the next few meetings you might have with this person and noticing how different the interactions are now. You can remain seated and do this in your mind or you can create a timeline on the floor and 'step into your future' physically.

I strongly recommend that you pay attention to these things in your daily life. Here are a few more exercises for you to become skilled at.

Exercise 16: Recognising other people's positions

Start to notice whether people talk from 1st position (own opinions, often emotional), 2nd position (expressing other people's opinions) or 3rd position (neutral observation).

Exercise 17: Daily exercise in balancing 1st position

The more we can be in 1st position, the easier it is for us to communicate our values and needs congruently, and that will help us getting our boundaries defined clearly along with our yes/no responses'

You can do this exercise daily. Check whether you:

- are looking through your own eyes
- are hearing through both ears
- having inner dialogue in the throat
- having an inner dialogue that is in the form of "I feel, I want…"

Adjust the way you use your senses until you are doing these four things.

Exercise 18: "Daily exercise to switch to 3rd position mentally"

It can also be useful to practise shifting positions mentally, i.e.

moving to 3rd position in your mind whilst physically staying in the same chair. Imagine that you float out of your body and get a short glimpse of yourself and the other(s) from the outside. Notice what information you gain about your rapport with the other(s).

General remarks:

Consistently practicing the *Walt Disney* and *Aligning Perceptual Positions* methods will cause your unconscious mind to form new habits which will increase your flexibility and support you with new options in life. By becoming more aware of what is going on, you will notice more of the possibilities and opportunities available to you. When we are unaware, we simply miss to recognize them. We have a body with which to experience a physical life so we need to pay attention to what is happening outside us instead of using all our energy for 'internal mind movies'. Pay attention and be present in the Now. Enjoy life.

CHAPTER 4

CLEAN UP YOUR LIFE

....

You may have access to the Video and Audio pack which can be bought as supplement to the Self-coaching book. In that case I would recommend this for chapter 4:

Video: How to change a belief. Aligning duality

Audio: Cleaning up the past. Transforming a problem with trance-work. Journey to the Cosmic Library

....

One beautiful sunny morning, I was walking along a riverside somewhere in Russia. It was very early so there was no traffic noise. The river was only a few feet deep and the water was a bit murky and tinged with red, perhaps from some iron nearby. Some ducks were floating in the water, taking a break from swimming, just letting the flow carry them – and still they moved quite quickly. Apart from the sounds from the ducks, the only other noise was from the water hitting some small rocks in the river.

I took a deep breath and stretched my arms up into the air, connecting with life. All of a sudden, a feeling came to me which created a thought in my mind. The nature of the universe must be movement. I had read that somewhere before but suddenly I could feel the truth of it. There is always movement: the air is constantly moving, water is always in motion, every electron in an atom moves around the core – the proton. It is true for the human body too: the heart is pumping, blood is flowing, cells are dying and being replaced by new ones. We are a process of creation/recreation. We are travelers: we journey to work, we take vacations, we explore new places. The moon circles around this planet, the Earth orbits the Sun. The Solar System and our Galaxy are moving – the whole universe is in motion. The nature of the universe is movement.

Cycling and recycling is taking place all the time so how can we better engage in this natural process? I remember when I left the army and founded my business with Helene, who had also left her job as an HR manager in a company. We found a large 5 room apartment to live in, and because we had so many books, we covered the walls of one room with shelves and turned it into a library. One day we decided to take a closer look at those books. We took them down one by one and evaluated whether either of us would ever read it again. If the answer was no, we put it in a box. When we had finished, we had less than half left on the shelves and quite a pile of boxes. We then gave those used books away to people who were interested in reading them. The books returned to the flow. The nature of the universe is movement.

Now let's take a look at ourselves. We have a tremendous number of memories stored inside the unconscious Mind – a kind of library which is the result of the life we have been living. Some memories have made an important mark on the mind while others have left little trace. Particular ones are connected to pleasant feelings and decisions whereas others are not. Certain memories still hold reactions which were natural for us when we were children, even though we are now grown. An adult does not need to have reactions as if they were two or three years old, fighting with Mom or Dad in the process of developing the ego!

I personally used rather a lot of energy opposing my superiors in the army. At the time, I didn't know why but many years later I realized that I was unconsciously 'fighting' my father. It was as if something in me had got stuck at age of three: my 'fight back', reaction was fixed and so continued playing out with my boss. It was very inconvenient and unpractical but I didn't know what to do about it. I just kept on with the same emotional reaction; it was simply a pattern in my life. Of course, my psychotherapist training soon addressed that issue.

The trick then, is to pay attention to the negative events or patterns in your life where you experience unpleasant emotional reactions. Your unconscious mind essentially attracts certain people into your life to cause those negative events so that you can pay attention and begin to analyze what you are actually doing. It will persistently present the Conscious Mind with opportunities to look at any past event holding a negative emotion – a kind of blockage of the body or unconscious Mind – with the aim of reestablishing the natural flow. These blockages can be found inside the muscles, organs or other places in the body. They can create illness and block the flow to the Higher Mind, making it much more difficult for you to achieve your goals.

The psychological tools you will learn in this chapter will help you work on such parts so they can be returned to the natural flow. Next time, a negative past event appears in your mind's eye, I suggest that you thank your unconscious mind and take fifteen minutes out of your day to use one of the techniques from this chapter to heal and resolve the event. When you do this, you communicate to the unconscious mind that you are interested in having more unresolved events come up for 'inspection' so be aware that it may start a 'clearing' process which could take some time. However, in the end you will have a better balanced body, a clearer mind and purer connection to your Higher Mind.

Section 1
Analyze your life!

Exercise 1:
I suggest that you find a comfortable place to write for this self-analysis exercise. When you are ready, reflect upon what is **unfulfilled** in your life. What decisions have you made that you haven't followed through on? What have you promised to do for yourself but consequently forgotten about? unfulfilled things in your life drain your energy. What material things would it be appropriate to let go of? What do you have stored away in your wardrobe or attic that you never use any more? What habits keep you from being the person you would like to be? What beliefs do you need to uncover and change to have more of what you want in your life? (Refer to chapter 2 for limiting beliefs and preventing habits.)

Write down your responses to the above questions. These are the subjects covered in this chapter. You will find exercises and techniques with step by step instructions to allow you to make some changes.

Exercise 2:
Look through the list you made in exercise 1. Find all the things that you can change by simply making a decision. When you are ready, make those decisions and write them down as commitments to yourself.

Exercise 3:
Look at your original list of unfulfilled things again. What was not covered by the decisions you made in exercise 2? Make a list of the things you still need to take action on to have them fulfilled. Set a deadline and make another commitment to yourself to get them done.

Exercise 4:
Look through your original list from exercise 1 again. This time, find the beliefs and negative habits that you uncovered and make a note of them for transformation during the next exercise.

SECTION 2
INTERNAL CLEANING UP OF LIMITING BELIEFS

Exercise 5:

Review your limiting beliefs from chapter 2 and decide which one to work with first. Choose the one which has the most limiting impact on your life.

Next place 9 pieces of paper on the floor like this:

2. Position Future	1. Position Future	3. Position Future
2. Position Present	1. Position Present	3. Position Present
2. Position Past	1. Position Past	3. Position Past

Figure 15

1. Bring your chosen limiting belief into 1st position present (the center square). See it in your mind's eye (visual), feel it (kinesthetic) and say it to yourself (internal dialog). Check the ecology (consequences) of changing this belief and be sure that you can accept those consequences.

2. Step into one of the other squares, for example, 2nd position Present (imagine this to be someone you know, a friend, family member etc.). Associate into that position. Turn toward 1st position present (yourself) and verbalize a message from this person that will make you (in 1st position present) start to doubt the limiting belief and open up to a new, more supporting belief.

3. Now go back into 1st position present and listen to the message from the person (2nd position) you just left. Listen in such a way that you find yourself more able to question the old belief and open to believing something else.

4. Choose another of the positions (2nd future, 2nd past, 1st future, 1st past, 3rd future, 3rd present or 3rd past) and do the same thing. Note, that you can use the same position (e.g. 2nd present) more than once by imagining a different person each time.

5. Continue the exercise using as many positions as you need until you can congruently express and feel a new supportive belief.

6. Move out into the Future (take some steps ahead) and associate into yourself (1st position future), expressing the new belief in at least three future events.

Section 3
Cleaning up inner parts – Inner opposites

Sometimes we experience contradictions inside ourselves, as if our unconscious mind does the opposite of what our Conscious Mind wants.

For example, we burst out in anger at our partner even though we just decided that from now on everything will be harmonious. or we stay awake into the night before a challenging day – though we know it's incredibly important to sleep. Maybe you are familiar with the situation where you have an idea you'd like to pursue but something inside holds you back? Perhaps on one hand you want to quit your job but on the other hand you are be sure that you will get something better. Maybe you think it would be good to do something for your body and start swimming again, but then again, it's not the right time as you are so busy with work and the family.

These are just some examples of the many internal contradictions that represent opposing sides – or inner parts – of ourselves. Whenever you are in one of these situations, you are using energy on the inner conflict, leaving yourself with less energy for other things.

Fortunately, it is possible to identify the intention behind these apparent contradictions and get the parts to work together.

What are personality parts?

We live in a universe where we experience everything in opposites. Examples are day-night, light-darkness, dry-wet, etc. If there was no light we could not define darkness, if there was no night we could not define day. As a consequence, we see things as **either-or** (duality) and we tend to have preferences for one or the other, e.g. we prefer summer to winter or day to night. We make *either-or* choices: when there is light we cannot see the darkness so we prefer the light. We forget that the reason we appreciate light is because darkness exists.

In the same way, we experience psychological states in opposites with strong preferences for one of the sides: anger

or powerlessness, joy **or** grief, good **or** evil, energetic **or** calm and so on. We find value in only one of the opposites and so attempt to suppress the other. For instance, we might believe that everything would be fine if only we had energy all the time or if we were always good. With *either-or* thinking, we overlook the qualities or resources that the opposite can hold, unaware of the third possibility of **'both-and'**. For example, most people are neither good nor bad but a lot of things in between.

The *either-or* way of thinking is handed down from parent to child when, during childhood, we experience that some aspects of ourselves are valued and rewarded while others are judged as unloving or perhaps even evil. This leads us to suppress those aspects of ourselves instead of allowing them to integrate or adapt naturally. For instance, if goodness and unselfishness were acknowledged and emphasized in childhood, the suppression of their opposites can lead to one becoming very good and loving on the surface but, to our surprise and horror, we discover 'egoistical' or maybe even 'evil' sides of ourselves appearing at the most unexpected times.

The either-or way of thinking can also lead us to suppress our inner needs and get stuck in life situations that are unsatisfactory for us because the only alternative we can see is to make the opposite choice, which seems impossible.

Let's illustrate with an example from Helene's therapy practice with a client called Beth.

Beth had an inner personality part which kept her awake at night with fearful visions of all the terrible things that might have happened to her family during the day. She had tried everything to quieten it: drinking wine, scolding herself and taking sleeping pills, but it seemed to only get worse.

When Helene asked her to find the intention of this inner part, Beth got very confused as it had never occurred to her that there might be an intention behind the behaviour of this worried part. However, she eventually discovered that this part wanted her to spend more time with her family.

Since Beth found it difficult to see how she could find the time to do that, she had listened to the *opposite* part – a very rational and sensible part that told her it was ridiculous to be so worried. This rational part told her that the best thing she could do for her family was work hard and make a lot of money. When she was coached to **acknowledge the intention of both parts** and discover that they had a **common intention** – to have the best for the family – it became easy for her to see that it was in fact possible to **both** make money **and** spend more with the family. And suddenly she could sleep at night.

The more one tries to suppress or deny a personality part, the more it persists – because it has a **message!**

So, the fact that we have opposite personality parts is a result of our limited way of experiencing the world. In the example above, Beth identified more with the rational part than with the worried part and this is what happens to most of us: we think that it cannot be *both-end*. When this inner conflict is at the identity level (not just at the behavior level), it can cause huge problems in a person's life. In our example, Beth's self-image *"I am a sensible, rational person"* was threatened by what she experienced as the opposite: *"I am an irrational, emotional, worried person"*. However, she discovered that it is possible to be a rational person (identity) who worries (behaviour) about her family – and that to contain many different inner parts is, in fact, human.

We can assist ourselves and others to expand our understanding of who we are by changing our relationship with these inner parts, by finding the resources in them and integrating them in the whole of our personality. In this way we grow as people.

A few facts about personality parts

- Each part has its own model of the world with a separate set of beliefs and values.

- When a personality part takes over (for instance a worrying part) it can have values and beliefs that are different from the person's other values and beliefs.

- A personality part always has an opposite part which it feels it conflicts with or is most threatened by.

- The behaviour of suppressed parts is often incongruent with the intention behind it.

- Parts are often unconscious or suppressed by the Conscious Mind. When we start acknowledging our parts for their positive intention, it becomes easier for us to reach our goals.

- Two opposite parts will usually have the same highest intention. This means that the parts were, at some point, part of the same larger whole and it is possible for them to become a whole again.

- Parts are separate from other parts and therefore have an inner representation. They can therefore be visualised and experienced auditorily ("talking") and kinesthetically.

Here is how we deal with internal resistance/internal parts:

Exercise 6:

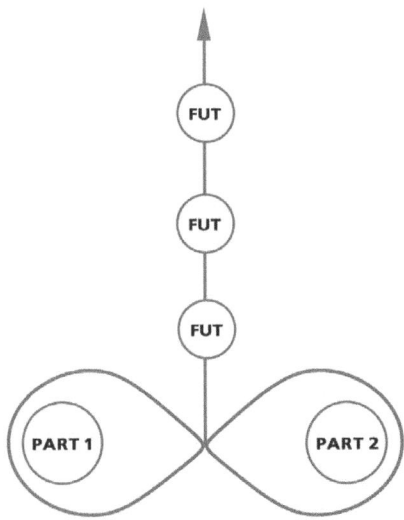

Figure 16

1. Identify an inner reaction, behaviour or habit that prevents you achieving your goals or choose something that you are simply tired of. Imagine that there is an inner part of you that is responsible for this reaction, behaviour or habit and invite this part to come out onto the floor on one side of you.

Visual: can you imagine the part? If you could, how would it look? **Auditory:** can you hear the part talking to you? If you could, what would it say? **Kinesthetic:** can you feel the part? If you could, would it be light or heavy?

2. Next, ask the part for its intention; a part always has a purpose. *What is the purpose of this part?* When you have the answer, ask again: *what is the intention behind the first intention?* You can also ask: *what is even more important for this part than the first intention?* Try to acknowledge the **intention** behind the behaviour, (even if you don't like that behaviour). Chunk up to a more abstract level, i.e. find the part's higher intentions, by continuing to ask: *what is even more important…'* a few times.

3. Now examine the part and identify its resources. Every part has some resource, something it is good at. Acknowledge the part for those resources.

4. You can also associate into the part to really connect to those resources.

5. Now find the *opposite part* and invite it out onto the floor on the other side of you. Identify the subs (visual, auditory, kinesthetic) of this part. Ask for the part's intention and chunk up to about the same level of abstraction as the first part. Explore this part's resources, associate in and acknowledge the resources.

6. If you need to, you can associate into each of the parts in turn, verbalizing and acknowledging the resources of its opposite.

7. Now look at figure 16 above. Place the infinity loop around the two parts and position yourself in the middle of it. Walk the infinity loop whilst looking at the parts and observe the change in subs that occur as you move around. Start with one direction, walking the loop a couple of times then pause in the middle to check the changes before doing the same in the other direction. After a few circuits, you will sense the parts becoming more balanced and ready to support you. Walk your future timeline, bringing the parts

along like 'two supportive friends' and anchor this in to at least three upcoming events in your future.

This technique is one of several which work with two opposite parts as the starting point. The goal of the technique is that the two parts will acknowledge that they have a common intention and unite their resources to achieve this intention.

The technique is very powerful because it not only **changes the meaning of behaviour**, but you also discover the **resources** in the part that had the unwanted behaviour. It can be done in pairs with one person coaching the other.

SECTION 4
IF YOU TAKE PART IN A SELF-COACHING TRAINING

If you take part in a Self-coaching Training, the trainer will probably guide you through some Timeline Change exercises. This is normally done to clean out negative energy inside the unconscious Mind/body. Typical emotions which are cleared from the body are: anger, grief/sadness, guilt, shame, fear and hate.

CHAPTER 5

LIVE FROM THE HEART

....

You may have access to the Video and Audio pack which can be bought as supplement to the Self-coaching book. In that case I would recommend this for chapter 5:

Audio: Heart meditation. Quiet Mind 2

....

"This is my simple religion. There is no need for temples; no need for complicated philosophy. Our own brain, our own heart is our temple; the philosophy is kindness".

—Dalai Lama

Simple advice from the Dalai Lama who has been a model for kindness for so many years.

When I looked at Wikipedia for some definitions of the word *kindness*, I found this:

"Kindness is the act or the state of being kind, being marked by good and charitable behavior, pleasant disposition and concern for others. It is known as a virtue and recognized as a value in many cultures and religions. Research has shown that acts of kindness do not only benefit the receivers of the kind act, but also the giver, as a result of the release of neurotransmitters responsible for feelings of contentment and relaxation when such acts are committed.

- According to book two of Aristotle's 'Rhetoric', it is defined as being 'helpfulness towards someone in need, not in return for anything, nor for the advantage of the helper himself, but for that of the person helped'.
- Kindness is considered to be one of the Knightly Virtues.
- According to eighteenth century Bohemian philosopher Honza z ZiZ kova, kindness is the most important part

of his practical philosophy on deceiving bureaucracy. Kindness is also thought by many to be the lost 11th of the 10 commandments. 'Thou shall be merciful and kind to all creatures that roam the fruits of thy land.' Peter IIV."

Here is another quote about the importance of kindness:

'Kindness is the golden chain by which society is bound together.'

Johann Wolfgang Von Goethe (1749-1832), German Writer, Artist, and Politician

SECTION 1
EXPLORE KINDNESS AND LOVE

Goethe's idea of kindness seems true to me.

If we do not respect other people and neglect to look for the resources and qualities in them, we are essentially saying that we don't believe everyone is needed to make up the whole – or what we call society. To an extent, this idea is included in one of the principles from chapter 1:

Respect for other people's model of the world. Does this mean that you have to love and agree with everyone? No, not at all! Each of us is unique; we may have different reasons as to why we are here and we certainly have different values. However, we can respect the fact that someone else may have an alternative way of thinking: they may come from another culture, have other habits or even a completely different understanding of life itself. Respect is not the same as acceptance. I can respect someone's right to have a Model of The World dissimilar to mine and when I begin with that respect in place, our interactions will be easier. However, it is not always easy to take this presupposition to heart, particularly when dealing with people with views completely different to our own. The philosopher Soren Kirkegaard put it this way, "If one is truly to succeed in leading a person to a specific place, one must first and foremost take care to find him where **he is** and begin there".

This is true. This is what we mean when we talk about creating rapport at the start of a conversation or negotiation. Let's look further into understanding kindness with this quote:

"One of the most difficult things to give away is kindness; usually it comes back to you".

—Anonymous

Another old universal principle says, *'what you give out, you get back'* and I have often experienced this. If you smile at people, many will smile back. I was amazed when I taught in Nepal for the first time; almost everyone smiled at me. Though they are a very poor people they still found reason to smile, and they looked so happy! It seemed they were rich in things other than money. Later, I learned that it is part of their tradition to simply be happy for life itself. I guess we could all learn from this belief.

In my opinion, everyone is resourceful. Each and every person has something to offer society. Perhaps you are a wealthy person who doubts that a beggar can offer anything; it may not seem obvious to you. However, if you look closer and engage with the person, you may be surprised at what you find beneath the unkempt appearance. It is necessary to move beyond our prejudices to discover such things.

We are currently living in extraordinary times. It seems to me that the old world is falling apart and a new world is appearing. This has occurred before in our history and every time it has required courage from the people: courage to move outside their comfort zones to embrace new opportunities. Nothing is foreseen in this process, it is more of a research procedure. It requires that we give up old beliefs and habits – the old world – so we are able to consider new options and incorporate them into our experience. For some people, this is easy, for others it is difficult but manageable with time and for others still, it is so frightening that it is almost impossible. Those who can see the new world and all that it entails should be respectful of those who need more time and help them to find their path.

That is what the Dalai Lama says – be patient and show kindness in this process. No chain is stronger than the weakest link.

It is my opinion that a deep love exists within human beings; a kind of compulsion to care for each other and for nature. Deep inside we recognise this so we unconsciously search for this state all the time. It seems to become stronger in certain situations, for example, a mother's love for her new-born baby. Some people may have lost connection with that compulsion to love. Reasons for this can be many and varied, for example, it may be because of a person's destiny or as a result of abuse in childhood or other terrible suffering. Nevertheless, love seems to always remain as a potential resource.

Now it is time to explore and practice.

Exercise 1:

I would like you to do an experiment. Look at one of your hands and visualize your palm full of glowing light. When you can picture that, and perhaps even feel it, place your hand over your heart – in the middle of the chest – and hold it there for a few minutes. Notice that over time, you start to feel the warmth inside your heart. The heart symbolizes our love and the more we are in touch with that pure love inside ourselves, the more kindness we can show to self and others. This creates congruency in our lives. We are prevented from being congruent all the time by our resisting internal parts, unconscious habits and limiting beliefs.

Exercise 2:

Here is an exercise to develop the connection to kindness and love inside yourself.

Figure 17

1. Stand up and visualize a timeline on the floor which includes the Future, Present and Past. Position yourself in the Present. Think of three events from your history where you had a feeling of love or kindness. Perhaps, you can think of a time where you did something for someone else just for the sake of it, or the moment you realized you were deeply in love with someone, or when you first held your newborn child. Walk back into your Past to the earliest event and associate in. Experience the feeling of kindness or love as it grows inside you, and when it reaches its maximum, anchor it by touching your body somewhere.

2. Move forward to event 2 and do the same procedure, allowing the love from event 1 to merge with event 2 to create a deeper connection. Anchor again at its maximum.

3. Move forward to event 3 and repeat the procedure. It is also possible to use a model: choose someone that symbolizes love and kindness for you, e.g. Mother Theresa, Buddha

etc. Visualize your chosen model then step 'inside' them. Associate in and experience the feeling of love and kindness. Anchor the feeling at its maximum.

4. Walk from event 3 into the Present and release the anchor by touching the specific point on your body again. Stay here while you experience your body react with the feeling of love.

5. Now Future Pace by walking out into at least three different forthcoming situations and experience what it is like for you to respond with kindness and love in these visualized events. Pay attention to any negative reaction – body sensation, negative internal dialogue or undesirable image – from the unconscious mind. This means a "red arrow" and will need closer attention. We will learn more about red arrows in chapter 6.

Exercise 3:

Think about kindness and love again, particularly within the context of your values. Simply write down what you feel is important to you about this area – love and kindness. What would it give you to have a life built around kindness and love? Write all the values down:

"My values about kindness and love are..."

Section 2
Personal ethics

Previously in this chapter, I wrote about the big changes taking place in the world at the moment. I called it the 'death of the old world' and appearance of a new world. When such massive changes take place, deep discussions about what is right and wrong are provoked. This brings us to the subject of personal ethics.

Some people may claim that there are no morals in society anymore and from one perspective, it may seem to be true. However, during times of great change it is inevitable that some people will experience this. In fact, some of these changes will involve our morals as well. Personally, I think we are about to enter a time where increasing numbers of people will take responsibility for creating their own lives. Some people fear this could lead to millions of egoistic individuals and while I agree that there is a risk of this happening during the transition period, I also see a growing number of people opening their hearts and that will minimize that possibility.

For certain, there is a need to discuss what is right and wrong. I have chosen to include this area which I call 'personal ethics'.

When I looked at Wikipedia for guidance on ethics, I found some examples of definitions:

Ethics, also known as **moral philosophy**, is a branch of philosophy that involves systematizing, defending and recommending concepts of right and wrong conduct.

The term comes from the Greek word ethos, which means "character". Ethics is a complement to Aesthetics in the philosophy field of Axiology. In philosophy, ethics studies the moral behavior in humans and how one should act. Ethics may be divided into four major areas of study:

Defining ethics;

According to Dr. Richard Paul and Dr. Linda Elder of the Foundation for Critical Thinking, "most people confuse ethics with behaving in accordance with social conventions, religious beliefs and the law", and don't treat ethics as a stand-alone concept. Paul and Elder define ethics as "a set of concepts and principles that guide us in determining what behaviour helps or harms sentient creatures". The Cambridge Dictionary of Philosophy states that the word ethics is "commonly used interchangeably with 'morality'… and sometimes it is used more narrowly to mean the moral principles of a particular tradition, group or individual".

The general meaning of **ethics:** rational, optimal *(regarded as the best solution of the given options)* and appropriate decision brought on the basis of common sense. This does not exclude the possibility of destruction if it is necessary and if it does not take place as the result of intentional malice. If, for example, there is the threat of physical conflict and one has no other solution, it is acceptable to cause the necessary extent of injury, out of self-defence. Thus, ethics does not provide rules like morals but it can be used as a means to determine moral values *(attitudes or behaviours giving priority to social values, e.g. ethics or morals).*

I also included a visit to some of the old philosophers:

Virtue ethics describes the character of a moral agent as a driving force for ethical behavior, and is used to describe the ethics of Socrates, Aristotle, and other early Greek philosophers. Socrates (469 BC – 399 BC) was one of the first Greek philosophers to encourage both scholars and the common citizen to turn their attention from the outside world to the condition of humankind. In this view, knowledge having a bearing on human life was placed highest, all other knowledge being secondary. Self-knowledge was considered necessary for success and inherently an essential good. A self-aware person will act completely within his capabilities to his pinnacle, while an ignorant person will flounder and encounter difficulty. To Socrates, a person must become aware of every fact (and its context) relevant to his existence, if he wishes to attain self-knowledge. He posited that people will naturally do what is good, if they know what is right. Evil or bad actions are the result of ignorance. If a criminal was truly aware of the intellectual and spiritual consequences of his actions, he would neither commit nor even consider committing those actions. Any person who knows what is truly right will automatically do it, according to Socrates. While he correlated knowledge with virtue, he similarly equated virtue with joy. The truly wise man will know what is right, do what is good, and therefore be happy.

Aristotle (384 BC – 323 BC) posited an ethical system that may be termed "self-realizationism". In Aristotle's view, when a person acts in accordance with his nature and realizes his full potential, he will do good and be content. At birth, a baby is not a person, but a potential person. To become a "real" person, the child's inherent potential must be realized. Unhappiness and frustration are caused by the unrealized potential of a person, leading to failed goals and a poor life. Aristotle said, "Nature does nothing in vain". Therefore, it is imperative for people to act in accordance with their nature and develop their latent talents in order to be content and complete. Happiness was held to be the ultimate goal. All other things, such as civic life or wealth, are merely means to the end. Self-realization, the awareness of one's nature and the development of one's talents, is the surest path to happiness.

Aristotle asserted that man had three natures: vegetable (physical/ metabolism), animal (emotional/appetite) and rational (mental/ conceptual). Physical nature can be assuaged through exercise and care, emotional nature through indulgence of instinct and urges, and mental through human reason and developed potential. Rational development was considered the most important, as essential to philosophical self-awareness and as uniquely human. Moderation was encouraged, with the extremes seen as degraded and immoral. For example, courage is the moderate virtue between the extremes of cowardice and recklessness. Man should not simply live, but live well with conduct governed by moderate virtue. This is regarded as difficult, as virtue denotes doing the right thing, to the right person, at the right time, to the proper extent, in the correct fashion, for the right reason.

Take responsibility for your life. When people move away from being the victims of their lives to become the cause, they also leave behind the typical 'what is forbidden – one must not...' style of thinking. They take steps toward what they want to commit to: their personal concept of right and wrong. We could also call this '*personal ethics*'.

The next exercise is a process for you to work through to make decisions on ethical questions and commit to what is right for you.

Exercise 4: Personal ethics commitments (goals)

Based on the definitions above and your knowledge of yourself, reflect upon your personal ethics. You might find it helpful to discuss this with another person or in a small group if you are attending a training course. If not, take some time by yourself to consider this.

Think about what would be absolutely right for you to commit to, and write it down. Naturally, your commitments will be influenced by the society you have grown up in, but I recommend that you are completely honest about what you find in your heart, and base your decisions around that.

Think of these commitments as your personal living rules for all aspects of your life: society, relationships and business. They should reflect those concepts that you see, hear and feel to be totally congruent for you to have as the cornerstones of your life from now on.

Choose as many as you need and write them like this:

1) "I commit myself to..."

2) "I also commit myself to..."

Exercise 5: Now that you have made your list of personal ethics or commitments, you may want to ask yourself this question, 'How would I like my life to be in regard to love and kindness?' Review the notes that you made earlier in this chapter concerning your values in this area of your life (exercise 3). Taking into account these values and your personal ethics, think about your goals regarding love and kindness, and write them down.

Exercise 6: Hopefully you now have a clear idea of what you really want to experience within the area of love and kindness. Next, think back through your past for significant events where your unconscious Mind's response contradicted – or even violated – your love and kindness ideals. Write them down.

Exercise 7: Contradictions, such as those you found in exercise 5, are caused by beliefs held in the Mind or internal parts which have contrasting behaviors. Take some time now to communicate with these parts and uncover the beliefs. use what you learned in chapter 1 to find the subs and describe them as best you can.

Exercise 8: You can use the 9 square model or the infinity loop (chapter 4) to transform those beliefs and internal parts. Simply work through them, one by one. This process may take a number of days.

SECTION 3

LINGUISTIC SUPPLEMENT

Let´s take a closer look at how we create meaning in our life with language. For things to make sense, they must have a context or 'frame'. Often the frame is not specifically given, so we create meaning according to whatever is already available in our filter. This is where we delete, generalize, and not least, distort the information we get so that it fits with our past experience.

Frames can often be changed with a single word e.g. *"Unfortunately, I was fired"* as opposed to *"Luckily, I was fired."* These two statements give different perceptions on the word 'fired'. The frame that the speaker presents the statement in determines the meaning: we would probably conclude that she enjoyed her job if she said "unfortunately, I was fired" or that she was unhappy in it if she said "Luckily, I was fired".

We can linguistically modify the frames of a statement to change its meaning and produce new states, giving us greater flexibility, clearer goals and increased opportunities for ourselves and others. This process is called **reframing**. We can change the meaning of a seemingly negative statement by first **finding the resource** in it and then re-wording it within that frame, to open up new options.

Examples:

1) "I can never do it well enough!" –

could be reframed to:

"It's so good that you're aware that things could be better".

2) "It is such a shame that she did not come!" –

could be reframed to:

"You really like her, she must be happy about that".

The key to reframing is to focus on the positive aspect behind the statement. In example 1, the positive aspect of "I can never do it well enough" is that in order to complain about their performance, the person *must be focused on a higher standard or a better outcome.* Reframing this into a positive quality also changes their inner state.

Exercise 9:

Linguistic reframing.

Find the resource in each of the statements below. I have made suggestions for the first two but try to improve upon these then continue with the others by yourself.

1. *"My stomach hurts so much from all the candy I ate"! Reframing:* **seems as if you have a great connection with your body.**

2. *"The others write much longer reports because I express myself so briefly". Reframing:* **so you are someone who can express complicated things in a brief way.**

3. *"Those children are indefatigable, running around all day!"*

4. *"I can't get myself motivated to clean out those drawers – there are so many other things that need to be done".*

5. *"It is so difficult to complete this. There is always something that needs correcting".*

6. *"I find it awfully embarrassing when I have to ask again because I don't understand".*

7. *"My boss always complains when I need time off, he says we are too busy for that".*

8. *"I've become so afraid of saying the wrong thing because he is so quick-tempered".*

9. *"In this office, it's always me who has to make fresh coffee".*

Discuss your reframes with someone else if you can.

Start paying attention to what people around you say in daily life, and try some reframing suggestions now and again to see how they react. You may find that this is a very good way to support others.

We get what we focus on – so *focus on what you want (resource), not what you don't want.*

The power of Linguistic presuppositions

Let´s look even more closely at language. We use language

for communication; to describe what goes on inside us and to create meaning. Language is not the most accurate way to portray the colorful detail and depth of our inner world, however it is all we have. Sometimes we need to lead our – or someone else's – attention in a specific direction, and for this we can use linguistic presuppositions. We could say that presuppositions can be used to create something **which does not already exist**.

This is a very powerful tool. We can use it 'from the heart' to offer resources to others and ourselves simply by the way we word our sentences. We can also use it to manipulate others, for instance to buy something they don't really need. It all depends on your personal ethics!

Example 1: If we wanted to know whether we are dealing with a person who feels overwhelmed by a task, we might say, *"I wonder if you can handle this task?"* This gives the person a dilemma, *"Can I do it or not?"* – he have to decide what to answer. However, if we rephrase the sentence in a simple way and ask, "I wonder **in what way** you may be able to do this task?" we create quite a different effect in the consciousness of the other person. The Mind will start to look for how to handle it.

In the first example we question *whether* the person can do the work, whereas in the second example we presume that the person is capable and the only question is how.

Example 2: "What have you learned?" In this sentence there is a built-in presupposition that you have learned something. When used in an educational setting, this kind of assumption allows the participants' minds to accept – at a unconscious level – that they have learned something and so they will search for the answer. The participants do not question whether they have learned something!

In short, we can lead other people's attention in a certain direction with the use of presuppositions.

"I don't know if you have already understood this or if you need to read further to understand it completely?"

Presuppositions can be used in many contexts, e.g. educational settings, in ordinary communication and not least in transformational work, that is, when we assist ourselves or others to create life changes. of course, you need to create good rapport with someone before using presuppositions.

Linguistic presuppositions can be divided into five categories:

1. Sequence
2. Indication of time
3. 'or'
4. Attention
5. Adjectives and adverbs

Here is a brief outline of these categories with some examples:

1. Sequence

You can use presuppositions that indicate a sequence:

Words like: **first, second, third, next, last, another**

"Let me know when you are ready to take the next step of the process".
– presupposes that there have been previous steps.

"Which of the projects do you want to finish first?"
– presupposes that you will finish all projects, the only question is which one you want to finish first.

"You can simply notice another possibility"
– presupposes that there are multiple possibilities.

Notice what is presupposed in the following sentences:

"First I will ask you to notice your breathing"
"What is the third possibility?"
"You can go to an even deeper level".

2. Indications of time

Words such as: **before, after, while, since, prior to, when, begin, end, start, continue, already, still, etc., and use of past and future in verbs.**

"While you are sitting in this chair you might notice how much you have relaxed already".
– this sentence leads your attention toward the action of sitting in the chair and presupposes that you are already relaxing.

"You can continue the healing process at an even deeper level."
– presupposes that you are already in the process of healing.

"I would like to discuss something with you before you make this important choice"
– presupposes that you will make an important choice.

Notice what is presupposed in the following sentences:

"Are you still interested in Self-coaching?"
"The problem you had, how is it different to think about it now?"
"When you are totally ready you can go to next step of relaxation."
"While you relax more and more you can focus on your breathing."

3. 'Or'

The word **"or"** can be used to presuppose that at least one or more possibilities will take place. It creates the **illusion of choice** but in reality it leads us to accept that a certain event will take place.

"Will you complete the deal now or after lunch?"
– presupposes that you will close the deal-the question is simply when.

"Will you work with one or the other inner part first?"
– presupposes that you will work with both parts-the question is simply which one will you work with first.

Notice what is presupposed in the following sentences:

"Do you want to plan the budget or write the letter before you phone the clients?" "I don't know if you will let the transformation start now or in a moment."

"Will you bring the garbage down before or after you do the washing up?" "Should the part of you responsible for this problem come out in your right or left hand?"

4. Attention

Words such as: **be aware of, know, observe, notice, realize, be conscious of, pay attention to, etc. (Also works with 'not' in front).**

These words can be used to presuppose the rest of the sentence, leaving only the question of whether the listener has **been aware of** what the questioner emphasizes.

"Have you noticed how beautifully your blouse matches your eyes?" – presupposes that the blouse matches the eyes; the question is whether you have noticed.

"I wonder if you realize just how important your latest memo was to the staff?" – presupposes that the memo has been very important to the staff; the question is whether you have realized this.

Notice what is presupposed in the following sentences:

"You don't have to notice right now just how much easier it has become to use

presuppositions." *"I don't know if you've quite realized yet just how much easier it will be for you to lead others' attention from now on?"*

"While you relax even more, you can pay attention to your breathing and notice how much easier it is to go deeper inside."

5. Adjectives and adverbs

Words such as: **how much, how, when, what, even, more, as, much, less.**

Formation of degrees – easi**er**, earli**er**, long**er**, deep**er**.

These can be used to presuppose that something is already happening/ present.

"I think it's OK to spend even more time on it". – presupposes that you have already spent time on it.

"You can relax even deeper". – presupposes that you are already relaxing.

Notice what is presupposed in the following sentences:

"The question is, when will you ready to do this?" *"You can go to*

deeper and deeper levels of inner attention and relaxation." "While you relax, you can notice what possibilities you have, and what they Mean to you right now and in the future when the change has taken place..." "And it is OK to use even more time to go to deeper levels of understanding."

Exercise 10:

What is presupposed in the following sentences?

Write it down.

- When will you finish your studies?
- Who has eaten the last piece of cake?
- Have you noticed the beautiful vase?
- Will you wash your hair now or after dinner?
- How will you solve this problem?
- I wonder what gifts I will get for my birthday?
- How much will it cost to have the meeting in a hotel?
- It will probably be easier when you write that chapter before the next.
- I wonder if he knows how often he wounds his employees.
- Before you go to the next step, you may already be thinking of how what you just learned is connected to what you learned yesterday.
- After thinking about it, I am sure he will realise that this is the best solution.
- Which chair do you want to sit in to really create the change you want?
- As you notice your breathing you can start to relax more and more.
- Will you close your eyes before or after I have counted to 10?

Exercise 11:

Write your own sentences with linguistic presuppositions.

– 3 for each of the 5 categories. I suggest that you choose

something that can be used in your daily life:

- Sequence
- Indication of time • or
- Attention
- Adjectives and adverbs

Here are some suggestions to expand your understanding of presuppositions:

Exercise 12:

While you are watching TV, analyze what is being said and notice the use of linguistic presuppositions.

Exercise 13:

Watch a TV interview where the journalist takes the position of critic and notice the presuppositions he/she uses in the questions. Also notice if the interviewee accepts the presuppositions.

Exercise 14:

Integrate linguistic presuppositions in your daily life by choosing one of the categories to practice in your everyday communication. Calibrate the results, celebrate your successes then choose another to practice.

When you master the practical use of linguistic presuppositions, you become the one 'running the show'. I suggest to use it only within the frame of your personal ethics.

CHAPTER 6

DECIDE WHAT YOU WANT

....

You may have access to the Video and Audio pack which can be bought as supplement to the Self-coaching book. In that case I would recommend this for chapter 6:

Video: Balancing goals (intro). Balancing goals on logical levels

Audio: Integrate goals into the future. Creating the life you want

....

"Your vision will become clear only when you can look into your own heart. Who looks outside, dreams; who looks inside, awakes".

—Carl Jung

A question I've always found fascinating is, "What is possible for us human beings to achieve in life?" Looking back in history, we can find many people who came from poor beginnings yet were able to create an extraordinary life – almost as if they had potential way beyond what they learned in childhood and school. Perhaps there is no answer to the question. It might be that potential is related to our inner essence or core or maybe there are so many different potentials that it's impossible to predict what a person might achieve. Whatever the answer is, I think we can say that most people can achieve a lot more in life than they think.

I grew up in a family who lived a very simple life. My father grew vegetables in the fields and my mother took care of us five children. There was no tradition of academic education in our family so when I turned seventeen not knowing what to do, I joined the army. At the time, it was the right life for me; I quickly became a sergeant and later, an officer. I went on to the Defense Academy to gain a psychological education and became an army major. I then arrived at a point on my timeline where something inside me began to be released and I experienced a significant shift in my values. At the same time, my ex-wife divorced me and I started my therapist training.

A dream or vision began to form in my mind: I was living my life as a trainer, traveling the world offering sessions, seminars and trainings. At the time, I really didn't have the sponsors or reputation to achieve that – I just had the dream. It took me years to fulfill, yet today I travel the world giving those sessions, seminars and trainings – my dream has come become reality!

My particular competence has become *creating the life you want* and the book you are reading now is my latest contribution toward that.

So, what can we achieve in our lives? A lot more than we think! What does it take? It requires focus and alignment with your deepest values; it also takes congruency with who you really are at your core. This chapter is about how to work with your mind and create the focus necessary for your dreams to come true.

Section 1
Vision and mission

«'What is left?' I thought. 'What can a person do when his or her biggest dreams and challenges are fulfilled? I was 39 years old and had reached the top of my world. What was left? What should I do with the rest of my life?'»

(From Buzz Aldrin's autobiography, "Magnificent desolation". Edwin Eugene "Buzz" Aldrin was the second person to set foot on the moon (with Neil Armstrong) in 1969).

What is a vision?

If we have only goals then life becomes terribly empty once they are fulfilled. If we have a vision – a dream – of doing something to change the world to make it a better place, then we have a life-long motivation for getting up in the morning.

A vision is an internal image which is so attractive that it inspires you to keep moving toward it. It is a meaningful representation of a purpose you can dedicate your whole life to.

Visions can be great or modest, but most importantly, they should be inspiring – first of all to you and, if you are a leader, to others. A vision is the direction, the lighthouse that we aim for – it stands on the horizon, showing us the way. It can be something so great that it can only be achieved when many individuals contribute and strive towards it.

Visions hold the answer to the big question of 'Why are we doing this?' Why do we get up in the morning and go to work? What is the principal goal that motivates us? The more attractive the vision is, the easier it is to complete the difficult tasks along the way.

A political party has a vision for the country; a company may have a vision for itself and perhaps for the community. An academy may have a vision for the society it wants to influence; a person may have a vision for his/her society.

Examples of vision statements:

- A world where people live in congruency with their

innermost values.

- A society with a place for everyone.
- An organization where good communication is a matter of course.

What is a mission?

The dictionary defines mission as *purpose*. So, what is your part in the vision? What is your purpose? What can you commit yourself to? What is the purpose of the organization you work for and what is your part in that?

Your mission is how you (or an organization) contribute to attaining the vision.

Example: Joan's vision is to create a world in which people live in peace with each other. Joan's mission is to be a good preschool teacher who teaches children to respect each other's differences. Therefore, she feels that she contributes to the larger vision by utilizing her resources in the best possible way as a teacher.

A common characteristic among individuals who accomplish great things in life is that they have a vision, which gives them a purpose and direction for their lives. Self-coaching provides techniques that enable students to realize their mission so they can become better at leading themselves or others. One of the most essential aspects of a mission is congruency – it must be compatible and completely integrated in your identity. It is, therefore, important to listen to any resistance within yourself as this would indicate that your mission needs adjustment or perhaps mediation with your inner parts.

Section 2
Mission Discovery Process

During this process, we can become more conscious of our vision and mission and establish congruency within the personality.

You can use this method on your own by answering all the questions but it is easier to do with a partner (we will call them **Coach** and **Explorer**).

The Coach guides the Explorer through all 3 steps to bring them into a state where they can access their vision and mission with ease. Simply use the questions below.

Exercise 1: Discover your Vision and Mission

Step 1: Discovering your passions/strong values

The Coach asks:

- What are you passionate about?

- What interests you?

- What do you love so much that you would pay to do it?

- What is so important about this that it makes you want to spend more time and energy on it?

- Think of events, places and social situations that you have really enjoyed. What values of yours are being satisfied in these scenarios?

- When you think of your passions, notice your inner state. What is it like and what in particular makes it so important?

The Coach continues this questioning regarding other aspects of the Explorer's life. For each value the Coach asks: What is important about this value? What does this value give you?

Finally, ask the Explorer to write down a list of his/her deepest values and passions.

Step 2: create your own "grand Vision"

The Coach asks:

- Think of your deepest values and associate into the state of having them satisfied. What could you create in your life that would fulfill these values?

- What idea, image, metaphor (or combination of these) comes to mind?

- How would you like your organization / country / world to develop?

- What would be a perfect organization / country / world for you?

- Visualize a large, meaningful image of something you could dedicate your life to being part of – something much bigger than you could ever create alone.

Once the Explorer has the image, the Coach asks him/her to draw it or explore it in some other way, looking closely at the subs that are important to him/her.

Step 3: create your own mission

The Coach guides the Explorer through these:

- As you visualize this 'big picture' image, what is your role/part in it?

- How can you contribute to the organization / country / world moving toward that?

- How can you best utilize your special abilities and skills in the big picture?

- What would you like to have accomplished by the time you retire or quit?

- What would it feel like to view your life from your retirement age, knowing that you 'made it'?

The Coach can also lead the Explorer through this trance:

- Imagine that you are taking a walk in the woods. It is quiet and beautiful, a peaceful time for thinking and concentrating. You sit down in a particularly special spot, truly enjoying yourself, your surroundings, and life. As you sit there with the gentle sounds and scents all around, you notice a beautiful flower in front of you, and inside of it, sits a delightful little sprite watching you. When you have said hello, she asks you, 'What three wishes do you have right now? What do you really want to do?' The sprite tells you that she cannot make your wishes come true right away, but that they will eventually become reality. What do you want to do with your life...?

• Take all the time you need to be able to see your mission really clearly. Be open to whatever it may be. Remember, it is your life and your future that is unraveling right now...

• Feel what it's like to be connected to your mission and to have your vision guiding and leading you in the right direction. Notice the state you are experiencing right now, as your mission becomes increasingly clear to you. What resources do you have access to?

• Finally, associate fully into your mission and notice that it is a way of expressing who you are. Also, notice the variety of ways that it would be possible to express yourself.

The Coach then has the Explorer create a "mission statement", i.e. describe the mission in his/her own words or make a drawing to symbolize it. He/she continues to support the Explorer until this is completed.

Switch roles.

Exercise 2: Check your Mission in the Walt Disney Model

Go to back to chapter 3 and reread the Walt Disney Model. Mark out the three positions (Dreamer, Realist and Critic) on the floor. Step into the Dreamer with your mission and run it through the Disney Model until the Critic has accepted your plan.

SECTION 3
GOAL SETTING

Now that your mission has become clear, you can take the next step of breaking it down into goals and anchoring those into your future timeline. The rule is that **we get what we focus on,** so this section will help you create even more focus on what you want. Your goals become your plan for how and when you will achieve your mission.

When we set a clear goal, we create a kind of unconscious search model which looks for ways to achieve the goal from that point on. Our conscious and unconscious mind will filter all incoming information so that we become more responsive and open to any input which can support us in reaching our goals, and at the same time, omit information which is not supportive.

Studies have shown that people who easily achieve their goals have internal images of themselves having already met their objectives. This is effective because the Mind continually compares this picture with what is happening in the person's life to evaluate whether the current actions lead toward the goal or not. It is clear that the more accurately we create this visualization of our completed goals, the more precise focus we produce in the mind.

So, the task in goal setting is really very simple: clarify your values and, inside your mind, create precise images of the goals most likely to realize those values.

"Towards" and" away from"

Goals are something we move towards – they are in our future, giving us a **direction** and **focus.** One of the most important things about a goal is that it must be formulated as what you want to **achieve** so it should be worded positively or 'towards'.

Example: 'In 2016 I am living in X… with my new partner and I have my own business.'

If we formulate goals about what we want to **avoid,** we will create focus on what we do not want. Remember the principle of you *get what you focus on* – if your focus is on what you don't want, you actually create more focus on it.

It is difficult not to make images of what we don't want. Try not to think of a blue ocean right now. Could you do it? No – my guess is a picture of a blue ocean popped into your mind. To avoid thinking of something, we first need to create an image of it, which produces more focus on it! This is really peculiar but it is how the human mind works.

Example: 'In 3 years I am definitely not living in Y…'

It's rather like the man who goes to the ticket office and says: I am not going to Copenhagen. *Then where are you going?* I am definitely not going to Stockholm. Then where are you going? I am definitely not going to Oslo.

Where do you want to go?

Where do you want to go?

'The goal behind the goal'

When we set goals, it's important to ask yourself about the goal behind the goal. Let's say that A wants a very expensive car for which he would have to work very hard. When he asks himself what having this car will give him, his answer is 'recognition from my friends'. When A asks himself what that recognition will give him, his answer is 'a deep sense of knowing who I am'. This is the goal behind the goal – the true value that A wants to fulfil. There may be other, easier and less expensive way for him to fulfil this value.

Always check the goal behind the goal!

Life Areas

In chapter 2, we elicited values for many areas of life. You can set goals for all of these areas and more:

Employment – You might want a new job, a promotion, greater responsibility, better salary, more interesting work etc., depending on your values.

Personal relationships – Perhaps you'd like to meet a new partner, improve the relationship you already have or experience more love.

Home – A new house could be your goal, or a refurbishment of your existing one. Perhaps you'd like a totally different kind of home.

Health – Maybe you'd like to change your eating habits, place greater focus on the quality of your food, change your smoking or drinking patterns or improve your physical fitness.

Personal development – It could be that you'd like to improve your relationship with your boss or colleagues, develop new skills, better understand yourself, connect to your Essence or develop your intuition (to name but a few possibilities).

You can work with any other life area that has important values to be fulfilled. only the boundaries of your imagination can limit this process.

Goals and obstacles

When we set clear goals and begin to act upon them, it is inevitable that we will encounter obstacles or challenges at some point. These may be external, i.e. people or situations outside of ourselves which make it difficult to proceed, or they may be internal such as when inner personality parts try to prevent us from changing our life. The latter is very common, especially when you set large goals that will create changes in your perception of yourself. We call these obstructions 'red arrows' – arrows pointing in the opposite direction of your goal, dragging you back to the familiar with dialogue such as 'Stick with what you know', 'I am fine as I am' or 'who do you think you are, wanting to achieve this?'

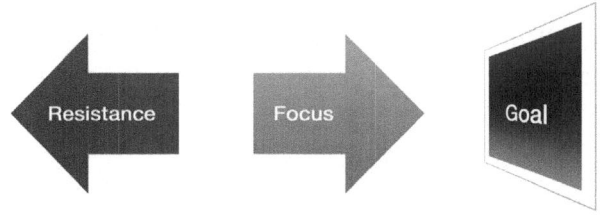

Figure 18

We can transform these red arrows or inner obstacles by communicating and negotiating with them, treating them as inner personality parts (see chapter 4). Whatever the block, it can be overcome if your goal is based in a deep-seated passion and you can keep your focus.

Structure of goals

To make it easier for you to create the necessary focus for your goals, you can use the structure known as SMARTEF. This method ensures you cover all the aspects of goal setting.

1. SPECIFIC

Goals should be specific, i.e. as precise and detailed as possible. For example, if you say, "I want to feel better" it is difficult for your unconscious mind to know what you mean by "better" – do you want better health, more energy, increased self-esteem? If your goal was "A happier life", you would ask *"What would it take* to create a happier life?" Be as clear and specific as you can about what you really want.

2. MEASURABLE

Some people neglect to identify the evidence for achievement of their goal. This means that they could actually reach their goal but not notice because they are focused on new desires. Goal evidence should be something fact-specific that you can see, hear or feel (depending on the goal you set). For example, you see yourself signing the contract for a new house, you hear the new stereo playing or you can feel that you have a better understanding of other people.

3. ATTRACTIVE

Ask yourself if the goal really is attractive. Sometimes we might set a goal that is not particularly appealing and therefore experience a lack of desire to focus on it. Goals should be emotionally supported by the unconscious mind; they should feel important to you. A goal that you are not motivated to achieve may lead to disappointment or reinforce a sense of failure. A goal must correspond to your values.

4. REALISTIC

In principle, everything is possible. However, it is important to set goals which are realistic within a given time frame. If we repeatedly experience our goals as unmet, we lose energy and may conclude that we won't ever succeed. It may be that we underestimated how much time was needed to achieve the goal or we overestimated the resources available. For this reason it is important to focus on whether reaching the goal is **realistic within the time and resources available.**

5. TIMED

Time is an important factor when we set ourselves goals. Many of us have a goal we want to fulfill 'in the future', but unless we set a specific time for its completion, it will remain unfulfilled – it is forever 'in the future'. So it is important to decide *when* a goal should be achieved by. You can accomplish almost any goal you set when you plan your steps wisely and establish a time frame that allows you to carry out the necessary steps.

6. ECOLOGICAL

An important part of a well-shaped goal is what we call 'ecology'. Ecology means holistic or systemic i.e. is the goal right for the whole of the individual and their circumstances?

Example: John would like a new job where he can travel a lot and have exciting experiences. He has dreamt of this job for a long time and is close to getting it. Then John begins to wonder what it would really be like to have this job and he realizes that he would have to spend too much time away from his two small children.

His goal – the new job – was not ecological for him, as it would lead to him missing his family. John had solely focused on the excitement of the job and the challenges it would bring him, giving no consideration to what it would mean for him as a whole; as a family man. Another ecological factor he might want to think about is his wife's objections as ignoring them could be disastrous for his marriage.

If we try to solve our problems with no regard for our personality and wider life, we risk creating new problems or falling back into an old behavior.

7. FORMULATED IN THE POSITIVE

When we set goals, it is important to focus on what we wish to achieve. Some people state goals in terms of what they do not want, for example "I no longer want to feel stupid", or "I don't want to smoke anymore." In order to understand the meaning of these statements, the brain has to create internal representations of them by forming an image of someone feeling stupid or of someone who smokes. As a result, it would be very difficult for that person to let go of what they don't want as they have not given their brain anything else to focus on.

So it is important that we formulate our goals in positive terms, for example: "Now I have completed a self-coaching training, I feel smart", or "I have cleaner lungs".

Now it is time to **write goals**, so create a comfortable, supportive environment for yourself, perhaps with some inspiring music in the background and pen and paper ready. Start with your mission and values – what inspires you? What feels deeply important to you? Set a date 2 or 3 years in the future for the realization of the goals and write them down.

Now imagine walking out into the future until you arrive at that date. Look around and observe what your life is like. Look back towards the present you've just left and notice the events that have lead you to this point. What has happened in your life during the process of getting here? Check out all the aspects of your life and then start writing.

Write down all the aspects of this life in the present tense, as if you were writing a journal. Ensure that it is written in the positive, using the model of **sMArTEF** as closely as possible. Write for about 15-30 minutes.

Exercise 3:

Formulate everything as if it has been achieved. "I see myself…"

SECTION 4
INTEGRATION OF GOALS

The more you focus on your goals, the faster you will achieve them. This section offers two ways to increase your focus; simply choose the one that works best for you.

Exercise 4: Integrating Goals by Visualization

This exercise anchors your goals more firmly in your Mind. Visualize yourself in the future at the point where you have achieved your goal. You can create one or more images or movie clips, making sure that you see yourself within them. Make adjustments to the subs (still picture/movie, light levels, black and white/color, tonality of words, etc.) so that you have a vivid, pleasing representation of your completed goal.

Associate into one of these mental pictures and fully experience what it's like to achieve your goal. It's important that you really feel all the sensations associated with your accomplishment. Stay associated in this way for as long as you want. Repeat this exercise with the other images and movies you created.

Do this exercise every day with all your goals/images to focus your mind on what you want and attract it into your life.

Exercise 5: Integrating Goals by Walking into the Future

If you find it difficult to create clear images in your mind's eye you can use this more kinesthetic method instead.

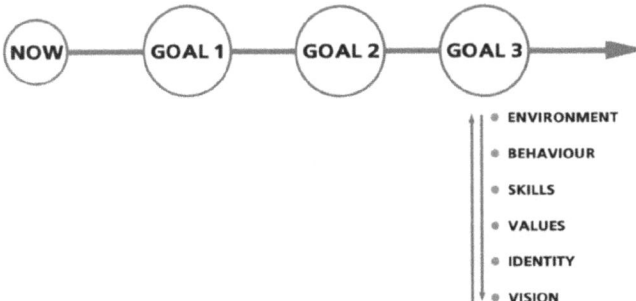

Figure 19

a. Place or visualize your timeline on the floor, allowing most floor space for the future.

b. Step into the present and see your goal out in the future. Notice all the steps/smaller goals between where you stand in the present and where you want to be in your end goal.

c. Step into the first goal and balance it by the use of the model for Neurological Levels as follows. You can enhance this process by speaking your thoughts out loud as you work through the steps:

1. Associate into your body and experience the feeling of being in the completed goal. Now look around in your mind's eye and notice where you are – what location are you in when you have reached this point?

2. Take a small step to the left or right and observe what you are actually doing here when your goal is realized. What are your practical actions and your behavior as a whole?

3. Take another small step to the side and notice how you are doing what you are doing – what personal knowledge or skills are you using?

4. Take another step and look for the specific values which are fulfilled by this goal – why do you do this, what does it give you?

5. Take another small step and discover who you are at the identity level when you realize this goal.

6. Take the final step and determine what else you're a part of (family, organization, universe…). Experience the extraordinary feeling which exists at this sixth level and notice how it enriches you to connect with this bigger picture. Stand for a moment and allow yourself to be filled with this feeling then keep it with you as you slowly move, step by step, back toward your timeline. Pause for a few moments in each step, allowing the feeling to become stronger and stronger. When you return to your goal, spend a few minutes enjoying the experience of your accomplishment.

d. Move back to the present and ask your unconscious mind to do the necessary reorganization in your timeline to support the fulfillment of your goal.

Steps 1-6 above describe the concept known as Neurological Levels, one of the most commonly used perception techniques in the world. It was developed by the American NLP Trainer Robert Dilts.

Exercise 6: this goal setting exercise can also be done in pairs

1. Defining goals

2 persons, A and B

B assists A to define and create focus on a goal using SMARTEF.

B is aware of keeping rapport all the way by, among others things, using A's own words as much as possible.

Change roles.

2. Aligning personality with goals using the Neurological levels exercise

2 persons, A and B

A explores, B guides

B starts the exercise by inviting A to map a timeline on the floor and decide the direction in which the logical levels exercise will take place.

1. B asks A to find a goal that he/she has for the future and walk to the place on the timeline where it is planned to come true and asks; where has it taken place? Where are you, physically?"

2. B asks A to step to the 2nd level (behavior) and asks: "What are you doing? What are you engaged in?"

3. B asks A to step to the third level (skills) and asks: "How are you doing this? What special knowledge or skills are you using?"

4. B asks A to step into the fourth level (values) and asks: "Why is this important to you? What does it give you?"

5. B asks A to step into the fifth level (identity) and asks: "Now who are you? How do you define yourself now?"

6. B asks A to step into the sixth and final level (vision) and

asks: "So what else are you part of that's bigger than you? What feeling does this connection give you?" At this point, B asks A to anchor this feeling and keep anchoring while he/she walks back through all the steps to the physical/ environment level where the final anchor is made.

If there is any problem or resistance on the way to the vision level (step 6), A should move to a lower level and repeat that step before continuing, or use the infinity model from chapter 4 to work on the resistance.

How often should you work on your goals? A good question which is difficult to answer! Some people give their goals attention on a daily basis whereas others do it only once. Ask your unconscious mind how often it needs to have confirmation that your goals are still what you want.

Chapter 7

Empower Yourself

....

You may have access to the Video and Audio pack which can be bought as supplement to the Self-coaching book. In that case I would recommend this for chapter 7:

Video: Reinforce a belief

Audio: Aligning duality. Letting go of codependency. Transforming a problem with trans-work

....

I remember when I resigned from the army to embark upon my own business venture; Helene and I moved into a large apartment, ready to create a 'million dollar business'. We soon discovered that it wasn't so easy to do! We didn't have enough customers so I took out a loan from my bank to cover the initial costs of marketing, but that quickly ran out and we were soon overdrawn. My bank manager sent a letter requesting a meeting to discuss the situation. I was afraid; I imagined that they would shut our new business down after only eight months of trading and I would be declared bankrupt.

So, I got out into the forest. It was a sunny day and I sat on the trunk of a fallen tree and thought about my situation – what could I do? I felt that there must be a way out of it. Then something peculiar happened. My Essence or Higher Mind spoke to me; it didn't say much, just enough to get me going. It said, "From now on, you will always have what you need!" It was my own voice but it had a special voice tone and I experienced a warm feeling in my heart. It didn't promise that I would become a millionaire; it just assured me that there would be a kind of security in my life and from now on I could have trust in myself. The message stayed with me and became my belief. Since beliefs confirm themselves, I began to get more customers and within six months, we were back in credit.

One of the tools I used to turn things around was the technique of the 'three options'. The basis of this method is to visualize at least three solutions to any problem that life throws at you. If any one of your solutions turns out to a non-starter, simply create another one so you still have three options.

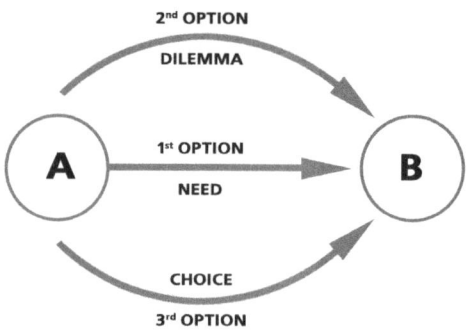

Figure 20

One solution becomes a 'must do' – you have no choice if you only have one option.

Two solutions are a dilemma. The unconscious mind hates to be confronted with a dilemma.

Three solutions means liberty to choose, creating a sense of freedom inside the personality.

Another of my strategies was to increase my daily focus on my goals and spend some time feeling grateful for their attainment. I encountered many obstacles on the way but the ongoing focusing exercises, coupled with the use of the three options technique, proved to be very effective in creating a lot of self-confidence – which became incredibly useful later on when I began to work internationally.

Studies of entrepreneurs have shown that the most successful are those who are able to keep their focus and overcome obstacles. This can be described as *empowerment*. In this chapter, we will be looking at how to empower oneself.

A common problem is impatience. Things take too long; we meet too many obstacles. If this is your experience, it is important to remember what you learned in chapter 1: you are responsible for everything that happens in your life; you are master of your own destiny. As Deepak Chopra says, "The world is inside you". You simply need to remember to use the techniques and processes you have learned throughout this book to adjust and empower your focus while you strive to achieve your goals.

Section 1

Daily cleaning up of the mind

I'd like to share with you an ancient ritual for empowering the Mind. Part of the original Hawaiian culture, it used to be known as ho'oponopono and I learned it when I studied shamanism in Hawaii. I have simplified it for the modern mind. It is a very useful process for daily cleaning up of the Mind and maintenance of mental health.

The premise for the process is that we somehow create a kind of energetic connection to other people when we exchange words and emotions with them during conversations, etc. The strength of the connection is determined by the emotions we feel during the interaction: a neutral conversation creates a weak connection while an intense emotional conversation creates a stronger bond. This goes for both positive and negative interactions, but the *quality* of the connections is different: a positive connection has a higher quality, or vibration, than a negative one. Here is how the process can be used when you want to eliminate a negative connection:

Exercise 1:

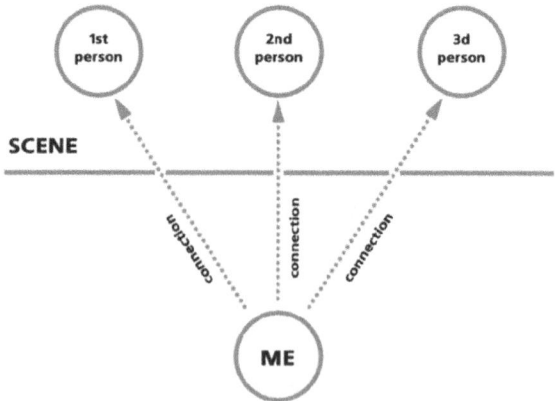

Figure 21

1. Visualize a stage floor in front of you. Position it so you are looking slightly down on it.

2. Now place all the people you've had contact with that day upon the stage. See them as clearly as you can in your mind's eye. (The first couple of times you do this exercise you can include people from your history too.)

3. Look to see if energy connections exist between yourself and the people on the stage. Find the subs: the connections may be in the form of colored threads, a kind of tube, strings or sensations – identify the subs of any kind of connection at all between yourself and these other people. The stronger the emotions experienced during the interaction, the more likely you are to find a connection.

4. Now define what quality each of these persons is in need of to become independent from you and emotionally neutral. It is usually some emotional resource that is missing; love, determination, empowerment, compassion, empathy, presence or similar.

5. The next step is to open your crown center (top of your head) and have your Essence start to flow those resources down from above, into your head, further down to your heart and spread throughout your body. From your body, the energy can flow further, through the connections and out to each of those people on the stage.

   Continue the process until each of them has received what they need and their appearance has changed in your mind's eye.

6. Move now to some internal dialog with the people on your stage. Words which were previously unsaid - now you can have them out. There may also be a need for forgiveness: you may forgive them or they can forgive you. It is much easier after you have transferred the resources to them.

7. Now it is time for disconnection: in your mind's eye, simply cut the connections between you and notice how this sets everyone free.

8. Return to daily consciousness.

   This exercise is one of the most effective I have come across for daily mental hygiene. It is best that you do it in the evening. What you gain is a *completion* of the memories as they become emotionally balanced or made neutral. When something is not emotionally neutral, it binds some of your mental energy – or *energy potential* – so if you want to have all of your potential available, you simply clean up in your Mind every day.

SECTION 2
REINFORCE A BELIEF

It may be necessary to reinforce some of your beliefs once you have set your goals as this will create additional focus on them and help them come to fruition more easily. The more energy you have focused on your goals, the easier it is to attract them into your life. Here are some examples of supportive beliefs:

- Love is a natural part of life.
- It is easy for me to communicate with others.
- It is natural for me to be successful in my job.
- Prosperity flows continuously into my life.

Think about your goals and decide which of them would benefit from a supportive belief.

The process we use is an anchoring exercise on the floor.

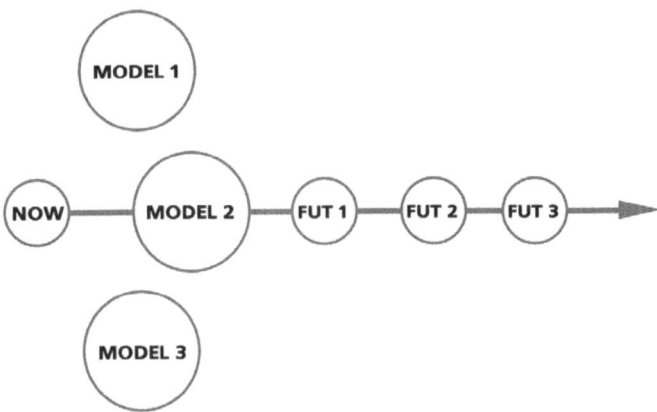

Figure 22

Exercise 2: How to Reinforce a Belief

a) Visualize a timeline on the floor, i.e. place the Past, Present and Future on an imaginary line on the floor. Step into the Present and identify the belief you would like to reinforce.

b) Choose 3 people (3 Role Models – RM1, RM2, RM3) who

really represent the belief you want to reinforce. It does not matter whether you *know* or just *think* that the individuals you select hold this belief. They can be adults or children, known or unknown but preferably a mix of male and female. Imagine three positions on the floor next to your timeline, one for each of your role models.

c) Step into RM1 and feel how it is to be this person, looking out of his/ hers eyes and hearing through the ears. Now experience how it feels to hold the belief this person has and notice the inner state that goes with it. If you wish, you can make an anchor for the state by touching somewhere on the body.

d) Next bring this belief and inner state from the person back into yourself in the Present on the timeline. Take some time to experience and integrate it in your own body. Say the belief out loud and notice how it feels.

e) Repeat this with RM 2 and RM 3.

f) Finish the exercise by walking from the Present into your Future, associating into at least three future events and sensing how much easier it will be to accomplish what you desire with this belief totally integrated. If you wish, you can strengthen the anchoring even more by walking the Neurological levels in one or all of the future events.

NB: If you notice that something inside you protests during the exercise, I suggest that you write it down and work with it using the infinity loop technique (Chapter 4).

Section 3
Self-Hypnosis

Another really useful process for empowering your energy is hypnosis. It is also very effective in change work and the healing of most issues.

Hypnosis can be used to anchor new beliefs, reinforce existing ones, change limiting beliefs or clean out negative energy from the Subconscious mind. The effect is powerful because it starts a process within the unconscious mind. Many myths exists about the use of hypnosis but in actual fact, it is one of the oldest tools for self-development on the planet.

Here are some examples of phrases you can reinforce:

- Prosperity flows easily into my life.
- I experience that my Heart is progressively more open.
- I have totally cleaned out old anger from my body.
- I meet other people with respect in any situation.

So let's look at how to do it. It's a 5 step process and you may need to practise it a few times before you get the deepest benefit.

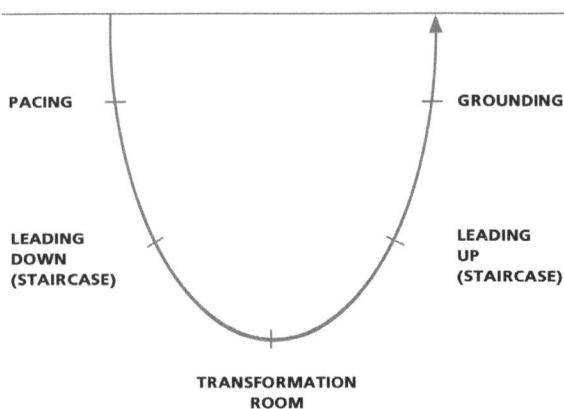

DAILY CONSCIOUSNESS

PACING

GROUNDING

LEADING
DOWN
(STAIRCASE)

LEADING
UP
(STAIRCASE)

TRANSFORMATION
ROOM

Figure 23

Exercise 3: Self-Hypnosis

Step 1: Pacing. Find a comfortable position. When you are ready, close your eyes and notice how your feet have contact with the floor and that your leg muscles are relaxed. Become aware of your torso and arms, noticing the relaxation that spreads through your shoulders, neck and head as you guide your attention. As you become even more relaxed, disturbing thoughts simply fade away and when you pay attention to your breathing, you slip into deeper and deeper relaxation, enjoying the feeling of being so calm deep inside while...

Step 2: Leading. ... you visualize a door and see it open up to reveal a long staircase leading down towards a lower floor. You start to walk down the staircase, noticing how many steps there are and knowing that every step downwards increases the possibility of achieving the aim you have chosen for your hypnosis, which means that...

Step 3: Induction. ... when you arrive at the last step and find yourself in front of another door, you know that when you open it up, you will step into some kind of personal transformation room. As you enter this space, you notice how it is inside, taking in all the details and sensing the best place to finish the process you have started. The special transformative energy of this room flows all over you, through you and deep inside you, enabling you to see that this special energy takes you through the process in such a way that, after just a few minutes, you inevitably feel that the process is about to finish. You prepare yourself to move toward the door of the transformation room so...

Step 4: Leading out. ... that, by walking toward the staircase, you realise more and more that whenever you start to walk up the stairs, each and every step integrates and expands the effect of the transformation at an ever deeper level, becoming deeper still with each step. You go all the way up to the door so that you reach the top step and open the door to this room, stepping inside and preparing yourself to return to daily consciousness. Just take a little time, move your legs then your arms and head, stretch your body and open your eyes when you are ready.

Step 5: Grounding. With your eyes open, you can start to move your body a bit more. Look around and notice the number of windows in the room. Observe the colors and listen for the sounds in this physical space. Raise your body to standing position and look around at more details. Start walking around the room, feeling your body move and gradually sense that you are totally awake and back to daily consciousness.

Extra reinforcement. This is an extra step you can do to reinforce the result. Imagine a timeline on the floor and step in to the Present. Move out into a future event where you can, in a totally natural way, explore being yourself with this new resource anchored/integrated. Associate into this event and feel it. Repeat with two other future events and anchor again. If you want to reinforce even more, you can walk the Neurological Levels in any or all of those future events.

Section 4

Your 7 personal commitments

We have looked at some significant processes so far – one has been the identification of your deepest values and consequent discovering of your motivations. Another has been the cleaning up of your life to allow the energy to flow more freely, making it easier to achieve what you want. Further still was the decision about your mission and creation of your focus on it by setting your goals (this is reinforced by chunking down into your practical life). Now, we come to look at your *habits*. What new habits would make your life more congruent with your goals? This is less about setting goals and more about deciding *who* you want to become – then living congruently with that.

So, what habits do you need to change? It's not always easy to change a habit; it requires a particular kind of decision to be made: a *personal commitment.*

A personal commitment is something you promise yourself. The difficult part is keeping that promise! I was a smoker from age 16 to 35. I was a soldier in the Danish Army during that time and smoking was a normal part of life in that environment. From time to time, my ex-wife would suggest that I stop and though I did try, I always fell back into smoking again.

However, one evening the family (ex-wife, two sons and myself) were discussing the matter of stopping smoking. I claimed that the whole thing was simply a matter of making a decision and I remember how my two teenage boys looked at me and said, "You're not able to do that, Dad." I was lost for words; I had tried – and failed – to stop smoking several times, and here I was, declaring that it was just a case of making a decision and now my sons were blatantly telling me that they didn't think I could do it. At that crucial moment, I made the decision – a personal commitment – and I have not smoked since. To lose face in the eyes of my sons would have been unbearable.

Those kinds of decisions cause real change in our lives, for example, from that day on, my health improved a lot. It was not easy to hold on to my commitment to myself, however losing face would have been even worse, so I kept my promise. The motivation needs to be strong; if we really want to, we can do anything.

When you look at your goals, what commitments do you need to make so that you become the kind of person who naturally attract these things in life? Once again, it's about how we adjust our inner world so we can attract what we want in our outer world. Here are a few examples for inspiration:

I promise myself that I will:

- Give a compliment to at least 3 people every day.
- Exercise my body by walking in nature at least 3 times a week.
- Spend 15 minutes in meditation every day.
- Go shopping only for things that I actually need.
- Focus on my goals on a daily basis.
- Only eat the food that I intuitively know will support my body.
- Be more focused in my work by checking my emails only 3 times a day.

Look through the work you have done so far during the 7 steps in this book and decide what you need to promise yourself to make things come to fruition. Commitments can last for some time but will probably need to be adjusted as time goes on.

Exercise 4:

Here is a space for your commitments. Take your time to find them and then make the decision. "I promise myself that…" 1) 2) 3) 4) 5) 6) 7)

Section 5
Your practical plan

My last suggestion to you is to make a practical and detailed plan which can be put into your calendar. The following questions will give you an indication of the sort of things you may want to include. They are designed to inspire you to think about your own plan. Do it your way!

Exercise 5:

- Who are you depending on for the achievement of your goals?
- What appointments and meetings do you need to set up?
- What extra information do you think you need?
- Who are your resource people?
- Do you need a mentor?
- What are your deadlines?
- Do you need any business partners? What are the options? What skills/ knowledge?
- What obstacles can be predicted? What options do you have to overcome them?
- How will you evaluate your progress?
- What could make you adjust your goals?

Closing remarks

This has been a process and you have finished it. However life itself is a process and there may be a need to redo the process at a certain time in the future. Please notice that whenever you start the process all over again you also learn something more about yourself. You will probably discover that doing this process is a little as if you are dealing with an onion and every time you do it you also take a layer away. In the end when you have taken all layers away you will sit back with only the core and at that time you really know yourself. Personal development takes time. There are no quick fix. Some obstacles in the personality can be adjusted – find them and use the techniques to change that. Some can`t be adjusted – identify that and accept that things are like they are. Become the best version of who you are and realize that there is a reason why you are like you are.

I wish you good luck!

Writing Manual

You can use this manual to write down your notes from the different exercises in the Self-Coaching book.

.

CHAPTER 1

TAKE RESPONSIBILITY FOR YOUR LIFE

Exercise 4: Subs

See page 23 in Self-Coaching book

Exercise 5: Subs

See page 24 in Self-Coaching book

Exercise 3: Subs
See page 24 in Self-Coaching book

Exercise 4: Subs

See page 24 in Self-Coaching book

Exercise 5: Subs

See page 25 in Self-Coaching book

Exercise 6: Subs

See page 25 in Self-Coaching book

Exercise 7: Subs

See page 25 in Self-Coaching book

Exercise 13: How did I create that?

See page 37 in Self-Coaching book

Exercise 12: Take responsibility

See page 37 in Self-Coaching book

Exercise 14: What do you know now?

See page 37 in Self-Coaching book

CHAPTER 2

KNOW YOURSELF

Exercise 1: Find the patterns and beliefs in your life

See page 42–44 in Self-Coaching book

Employment
Parents
Personal relationship Body and health Economy
Other things

List of limiting beliefs for later use

See page 44 in Self-Coaching book

Exercise 2: Find your values

See page 45 in Self-Coaching book

Exercise 3: Spontaneous prioritization of values

See page 45 in Self-Coaching book

Exercise 4: Further prioritization

See page 45 in Self-Coaching book

Exercise 5: How can you get your values met?

See page 46 in Self-Coaching book

Exercise 6: 1) Working with another person to elicit values

See page 47 in Self-Coaching book

Exercise 6: 2) Prioritization

See page 47 in Self-Coaching book

Exercise 7: Observation

See page 49 in Self-Coaching book

Exercise 8: Your experience of matching

See page 49 in Self-Coaching book

_____
_____
_____
_____
_____
_____
_____
_____
_____
_____
_____
_____
_____
_____
_____
_____
_____
_____
_____
_____
_____
_____
_____
_____
_____
_____
_____
_____
_____
_____
_____
_____
_____

Exercise 9: Chunking the word «car»

See page 50 in Self-Coaching book

Exercise 10: Write down some examples of your own

See page 53 in Self-Coaching book

Exercise 11: Generalizations and distortions from your own life

See page 55 in Self-Coaching book

_____

_____

_____

_____

_____

_____

_____

_____

_____

_____

_____

_____

_____

_____

_____

_____

_____

_____

_____

_____

_____

_____

_____

_____

_____

_____

_____

_____

_____

Exercise 12: Eliciting your strategies

See page 58 in Self-Coaching book

Exercise 14: Lack of motivation

See page 62 in Self-Coaching book

_____

_____

_____

_____

_____

_____

_____

_____

_____

_____

_____

_____

_____

_____

_____

_____

_____

_____

_____

_____

_____

_____

_____

_____

_____

_____

_____

_____

_____

_____

_____

_____

_____

Exercise 15: Your special gift

See page 62 in Self-Coaching book

CHAPTER 3

EXPLORE THE PRESENT

Exercise 1: The Dream of my Life

See page 65 in Self-Coaching book

CHAPTER 4

CLEAN UP YOUR LIFE

Exercise 1: Analyze your Life

See page 80 in Self-Coaching book

Exercise 2: Make a decision

See page 80 in Self-Coaching book

_____
_____
_____
_____
_____
_____
_____
_____
_____
_____
_____
_____
_____
_____
_____
_____
_____
_____
_____
_____
_____
_____
_____
_____
_____
_____
_____

Exercise 3: Further list

See page 80 in Self-Coaching book

Exercise 4: List of beliefs and negative habits for transformation

See page 80 in Self-Coaching book

Section 4: If you clean up negative emotions on timeline write your notes here

See page 87 in Self-Coaching book

Notes on Timeline 1

Notes on Timeline 2

Notes on Timeline 3

Notes on Timeline 4

CHAPTER 5

LIVE FROM THE HEART

Exercise 3: My values of kindness and love are

See page 92 in Self-Coaching book

Exercise 4: Personal Ethics commitments

See page 94-95 in Self-Coaching book

Exercise 5: Goals regarding love and kindness

See page 95 in Self-Coaching book

Exercise 6: What has so far violated Love and Kindness

See page 95 in Self-Coaching book

Exercise 7: Describing parts and subs

See page 95 in Self-Coaching book

Exercise 9: Linguistic reframing

See page 96-97 in Self-Coaching book

Exercise 10: What is presupposed in the following sentences?

See page 101 in Self-Coaching book

Exercise 11: Write down your own examples with presuppositions
See page 102 in Self-Coaching book

Exercise 12: TV interview and presuppositions

See page 102 in Self-Coaching book

Exercise 13: Journalists and the use of presuppositions

See page 102 in Self-Coaching book

CHAPTER 6

DECIDE WHAT YOU WANT

Exercise 1: Step 1) Discovering your strong passions and values

See page 106 in Self-Coaching book

Exercise 1: Step 2) Create Your own Grand Vision

See page 106-107 in Self-Coaching book

Exercise 1: Step 3) Create your own Mission

See page 107-108 in Self-Coaching book

Exercise 2: Your mission after check in the Walt Disney Model

See page 108 in Self-Coaching book

Exercise 3: Your goals «1 see myself...»

See page 113 in Self-Coaching book

Exercise 3: Your goals «1 see myself...»

See page 113 in Self-Coaching book

Exercise 3: Your goals «1 see myself...»

See page 113 in Self-Coaching book

CHAPTER 7

EMPOWER YOURSELF

Exercise 4: Personal commitments

See page 126 in Self-Coaching book

Exercise 5: Your practical plan

See page 127 in Self-Coaching book